UNEXPLAINED

Rupert Matthews

QEB Publishing

Project Editor:	Paul Manning/White-Thomson Publishing
Designer:	Tim Mayer/White-Thomson Publishing
Picture Researcher:	Maria Joannou

First published in the United States in 2011 by
QEB Publishing, Inc
3 Wrigley, Suite A
Irvine, CA 92618

www.qed-publishing.co.uk

A CIP record of this book is available from the Library of Congress.

ISBN 978-1-60992-133-0

Printed in China

Picture credits
Key: t=top, b=bottom, r=right, l=left, c=centre
Alamy Images David Wall 12t, 13; **Bridgeman Art Library** Private Collection 18, 28, Private Collection/The Stapleton Collection 51t, Brooklyn Museum of Art, New York, USA/Charles Edwin Wilbour Fund 52t, Christopher Wood Gallery, London, UK 56; **Corbis** Paul A. Souders 12b, Adam Woolfitt 3b, The Gallery Collection 41, PoodlesRock 46t, Hulton-Deutsch Collection 55, Homer Sykes 57b, Wayne Lawler/Ecoscene 69, Vo 75t, Trung Dung, Bettmann 94, Richard T. Nowitz 98, Theo Allofs 111, Wolfgang Kaehler 115; **F. Scott Crawford** 38b; **Getty Images** The Bridgeman Art Library 57t, Popperfoto 29, Aurora/Robert Caputo 81, Time & Life Pictures 92, National Geographic/Sarah Leen 97b, National Geographic 99, AFP/Stringer 108t, Mallory and Irvine Expedition/Jim Fagiolo 109, De Agostini Picture Library 112; **Images courtesy of RCN** 20, 21t, 21b; **Istockphoto** Ashwin Kharidehal Abhirama 26; **Library of Congress** 38t; **Mary Evans Picture Library** 104l, Paul Williams 106; **Photolibrary** Cusp/Peter Adams 73, John Warburton-Lee Photography/Nigel Pavitt 85; **Photoshot** UPPA 100; Dmitry Rukhlenko 113, Vitor Costa 114-115b; **Reuters** 87t; **Rex Features** CSU Archives/Everett Collection 9t, 62t, 74; **Science Photo Library** Tom Mchugh 72, Joe Tucciarone 80b, 31; **Shutterstock** Zens 2, 14, Eky Chan 3, Brian D. Meeks 8b, Christopher Poe 10b, KennStilger47 23, Vladimir Melnikov 26 (books), Sam DCruz 26-27 (background), Kletr 31, David Hughes 34b, 51b, Mikhail Nekrasov 35t, Sculpies 35b, 52b, Phillip Minnis 36t, Stargazer 37t, Vitor Costa 38-39 (background), Markus Gann 40t, Jose Ignacio Soto 40b, Tim Arbaev 42b, Jirsak 14, Paolo Jacopo Medda 46b, P.Zonzel 48, Stephen Aaron Rees 50, Homeros 54b, R_R 58, Stargazer 63t, Pichugin Dmitry 65t, Natalia Bratslavsky 66b, Andrej Pol 71b, Jeff Banke 75b, Ralf Juergen Kraft 76, Lijuan Guo 77, almondd 21t, Stephen Mulcahey 82b, Christopher Meder – Photography 83b, Adrian Phillips 86, Christophe Rouziou 91b, Rovenko Design 107, Igor Plotnikov 108b; **Stefan Chabluk** 36b, 53b, 90t, 97t, 110r; **Topham Picturepoint** Print Collector/HIP 10t, FotoWare FotoStation 11, 16, Charles Walker 17, Adam Hart-Davis 24, 25, The Granger Collection 30t, The Print Collector/HIP 39t, Mike Andrews 42t, 62b, 67, 78, 80t, 83t, 87t, Fortean/Healy 63, 65b, Fortean/Richard Svensson 64, Fortean 66t, 82t, 84, 102, The Granger Collection 90b, 110l; U.S. Navy National Museum of Naval Aviation 93t, U.S. Naval Historical Center Photograph 95 **Wikimedia Commons** 6, 7b, 31, National Media Museum 7t, 120, Library of Congress 8t, 19b, Admiral Horthy 15; Wikipedia M. V. Ingram's 1894 Bell Witch Book 22, 34t, 49, Andree Stephan 43, Marie-Lan Nguyen 45, Lyndsay Ruell 47, CaptMondo 53t, Mountain 54t, George Keith 59t, B Balaji 59b, 70, 79b, Dmitry Bogdanov 68, Department of Defense/US Navy 71t, 96, 103, 3bylunch 91t, Zaian 101b, Marie-Lan Nguyen 104r, ©Argenberg/http://www.argenberg.com/album/ 105; Wikipedia 114t

The words in bold are explained in the Glossary on page 116.

You can find the answers to the questions asked on these notebooks on page 118.

CONTENTS

THE
BOWMEN

≈ AND
OTHER
LEGENDS
OF THE WAR

BY ARTHUR
MACHEN

MARSHALL, HAMILTON, KENT & CO., Ltd.

GHOSTS

ARE GHOSTS REAL?

For centuries, people all over the world have told stories about ghosts. Some argue that ghosts are nothing but fantasy. But others firmly believe that ghosts are real. Read these pages and decide for yourself.

FACT OR FANTASY?

Many ghost stories turn out to have a simple explanation. For example, a house in the city of Bath in the UK was said to be haunted by the sound of a piano playing, until it was found that the ghostly music came from a piano two houses away. The sound had been carried by the water pipes!

 Borley Rectory in Essex was once known as the most haunted house in England.

HOAXES

Sometimes ghosts turn out to be **hoaxes** or tricks. More often, they are the result of **hallucinations**, when people see or hear things that are not really there. But not all ghost sightings can be explained away quite so easily.

INVESTIGATOR'S ESSENTIALS

Among the tools used by ghost hunters and paranormal investigators are:

Camera — to take photos and movies

Recorder — to record unusual sounds

EMF detector — to measure changes in **electro-magnetic** energy

Thermometer — to measure changes in temperature

Notebook — to record the time and place and other details of paranormal activity

 Victorian photographers often claimed to have captured ghosts on film. This photograph was believed to show a man being visited by the spirit of his dead wife. It was later exposed as a fake.

GHOST HUNTERS

When a witness claims to have seen a ghost clearly and at close range, ghost hunters or paranormal investigators will sometimes interview them and try to find out more. Often they will use cameras and special equipment to gather information about the ghost. If there is no scientific explanation, they may treat the sighting as **genuine**.

 Harry Price (1881–1948) was one of the best-known ghost hunters of his time and carried out many famous investigations of haunted houses.

A "classic ghost" always appears in the same place and behaves in the same way. Most classic ghosts are **apparitions** of people who have died some time ago. Sometimes they are even mistaken for real people.

INTO THIN AIR

During World War Two, British Prime Minister Winston Churchill was staying in the White House as a guest of the US President, Franklin D. Roosevelt. As he was dressing for dinner in the Lincoln Bedroom one evening, he became aware of a tall figure wearing a dark suit standing in the room.

Startled, Churchill said, "You have me at a disadvantage, Sir!" The man smiled and then vanished into thin air. Churchill later identified the ghost as that of President Abraham Lincoln.

GHOST FILE

Subject	Abraham Lincoln
Sighting	May 19, 1943
Place	The White House, Washington DC, USA
Status	UNEXPLAINED

 The White House in Washington D.C. is the official home of the US president.

Abraham Lincoln, born in 1809, was president of the USA from 1861 until 1865, when he was assassinated during a visit to the theatre.

FACT OR FANTASY?

When Queen Wilhelmina of The Netherlands stayed at the White House in 1948, she was woken in the night by a knock on the door. On answering it, she saw Lincoln's ghost staring at her from the hallway. She fainted and woke up later to find herself lying on the floor of her room.

Grace Coolidge, wife of US President Calvin Coolidge (1872–1933), often reported seeing the Lincoln ghost.

WHITE HOUSE WITNESSES

Churchill was not the first or last to see the Lincoln ghost. Other witnesses included Franklin Roosevelt's wife, Eleanor, and Maureen Reagan, daughter of US President Ronald Reagan (1911–2004). The Reagans' dog apparently refused to enter the Lincoln bedroom and often stood outside the door barking.

WHAT HAPPENED NEXT?

After each sighting, the White House was thoroughly searched for intruders, but no one was ever found. Since 1947, there has been only one sighting of the Lincoln ghost, but ghostly sounds are still heard in the White House to this day.

Who fainted after meeting the White House ghost?

When did President Lincoln die?

What did Winston Churchill say to the ghost?

Lady Jane Grey is believed to have been only 16 or 17 years old at the time of her execution.

Grim, gray, and forbidding, the Tower of London is one of the most historic castles in the UK—and one of the most haunted.

THE NINE-DAY QUEEN

In its long history, the Tower of London has often been a place of cruel punishment. It was here that Lady Jane Grey was imprisoned in 1553, after ruling England for just nine days—the shortest **reign** in English history. For seven months, Jane was held captive before being executed with her husband and father on the orders of the new queen, Mary Tudor. Her ghost and that of her husband are said to have haunted the Tower ever since.

GHOST FILE
Subject   Lady Jane Grey
Sighting   February 12, 1957
Place   The Tower of London, UK
Status   UNEXPLAINED

Built by William the Conqueror in 1078, the Tower of London was often used as a prison for enemies of the English king or queen.

GHOSTS OF HISTORY

Many other historical figures are said to stalk the gloomy nooks and crannies of the Tower. The wife of Henry VIII, Anne Boleyn, who was beheaded on Tower Hill in 1536, has been seen in the Chapel. Sir Walter Raleigh, executed in 1618, is said to haunt the Bloody Tower. The white-clad figures of two small boys, said to be the murdered nephews of Richard III, have also been seen there.

FACT OR FANTASY?

One evening in 1957, two Tower of London guards saw the strange misty figure of a woman in a long dress walking on the battlements. After several paces, the figure disappeared. The sighting took place on February 12—the exact date of the execution of Lady Jane Grey in 1554.

These two young nephews of Richard III are among the ghosts that are said to haunt the Bloody Tower.

Where was the ghost of Lady Jane Grey seen in 1957?

Who was the husband of Anne Boleyn?

Who are the two small boys who haunt the Bloody Tower?

CRIES AND WHISPERS

With its echoing **flagstone** floors, gloomy corridors, and gruesome exhibits, it is hard to imagine a creepier place than Old Melbourne Gaol in Australia.

 Cries of long-dead prisoners and sounds of ghostly footsteps are said to echo down the corridors of Old Melbourne Gaol.

PRISON GHOSTS

Built in 1841, Melbourne Gaol (say "jail") once housed hundreds of Australia's most dangerous criminals, including the outlaw Ned Kelly, who was hanged here in 1880. Between 1841 and 1924, more than 130 prisoners were executed, and many are said to haunt the Gaol today. Whether or not the tales are true, you certainly feel a shiver when you step inside.

 The **death mask** of Ned Kelly is one of many grisly items on display at the prison.

SHADOWY FIGURES

Since the prison was turned into a museum in 1972, there have been countless reports of ghostly figures, strange noises, and glowing lights. Many visitors have also spoken of feeling a sudden mysterious chill in the atmosphere.

One ghost believed to haunt Melbourne Gaol is that of prisoner "Lucy R," who committed suicide in 1865. Ghost hunters who spent a night in the prison on the anniversary of her death even claim to have recorded her voice crying for help from Cell 16.

When was Old Melbourne Gaol built?

Which famous outlaw was executed there in 1880?

When did the prison become a museum?

FACT OR FANTASY?

One night, the museum's **curator** was working late in his office when he heard footsteps, followed by scratching at his door. Stepping outside, he found the corridor deserted. No wonder he prefers to work when there are people around!

Hangings at the prison took place on this first floor landing where a **trapdoor**, known as the Hangman's Box, was cut into the floor.

GHOST TOWN, SOUTH AFRICA

The town of Port Elizabeth in the eastern Cape Province of South Africa is proud of its historic attractions. But inside its fine old buildings lurk a host of spooks and phantoms...

THE GHOST OF ROOM 700

In 1896, a fire broke out in the center of Port Elizabeth and a brave local policeman died fighting the blaze. When workmen started to build the town's public library five years later, they made the mistake of removing PC Maxwell's **memorial** from the site. For years after, his angry ghost was said to haunt the building. Happily, when the memorial was returned, the ghost of Room 700 was seen no more!

Scary apparitions, doors slamming shut for no reason, and books flying through the air have all been reported at Port Elizabeth's spooky public library.

FACT OR FANTASY?

One old house in Port Elizabeth is said to be haunted by the spirit of a young servant girl who was murdered by her lover. As a reward for good work, the girl was given the task of dusting the piano. People who lived there later claim to have heard ghostly music floating from the drawing room.

RESTLESS SPIRITS

Supernatural activity in a building is often linked with violent or tragic events that may have taken place there, such as murder, accidental death, or suicide. Many hauntings are also said to be due to "restless spirits"—ghosts who are sad or angry because their remains or final **resting place** have been disturbed.

GHOST FILE

Subject	Robert Thomas, caretaker
Sightings	Several since 1943
Place	Port Elizabeth Library, South Africa
Status	UNEXPLAINED

BANGING DOORS

Another person said to haunt the Port Elizabeth library is its former **caretaker.** For 31 years, Robert Thomas devoted himself to looking after the building. Even today he still goes around, banging doors, stacking books—and sometimes throwing them across the room!

The entrance of Port Elizabeth's fine Victorian public library.

Where is Port Elizabeth?

Who was the ghost of Room 700?

Whose ghost still haunts the library?

THE "ANGELS OF MONS"

Some tales of ghosts and the supernatural seem so far-fetched, it is hard to believe that people once thought they were true. One such tale is the "Angels of Mons."

MIRACLE RESCUE

On April 24, 1915, at the height of the First World War, a bizarre story appeared in the pages of a British magazine. It described how a supernatural force of "angels" had miraculously rescued a group of British soldiers during the battle of Mons, Belgium, in August 1914.

GHOST FILE

Subject: The 'Angels of Mons'
Sighting: August 1914
Place: Mons, Belgium
Status: DISPROVED

The story quickly spread. Suddenly everybody was talking about the "Angels of Mons." Not only that—according to the newspapers, even soldiers who had fought in the battle were saying the story was true!

 Soldiers who fought in the trenches during the First World War saw terrible sights that often haunted them for the rest of their lives.

BIRTH OF A LEGEND

In fact, it all began with the British writer Arthur Machen. His story "The Bowmen," published the year before, told how British troops at Mons had been helped by ghostly English archers from the Battle of Agincourt, France, in 1415. The story was meant to make people feel proud and patriotic—but it was never based on a real event.

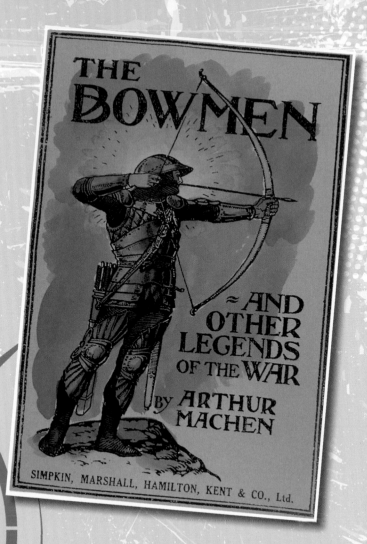

SIMPKIN, MARSHALL, HAMILTON, KENT & CO., Ltd.

Embarrassed by the spread of the 'Angels' legend, Arthur Machen always insisted his "Bowmen" story was just a piece of fiction.

FACT OR FANTASY?

The only evidence for the "Angels" story came from a group of Irish Guards who became lost during the battle, and were helped to safety by a woman with a lamp. There is no reason to believe the woman was a ghost, but her rescue of the soldiers may have helped to spread the "Angels" legend.

WHAT HAPPENED NEXT?

When Machen realized that he had started all the talk about "angels," he was horrified. He tried to explain that his story was made up, but nobody would listen. In the end, the story was repeated so often, everybody came to believe it was true.

What battle took place in Belgium in August 1914?

When did the story of the "Angels of Mons" first appear?

Who wrote the story "The Bowmen'?

THE FLYING DUTCHMAN

According to legend, the ghostly ship known as the *Flying Dutchman* was doomed to sail the seas forever, bringing death and disaster to all who saw her. Amazingly, this scary story is partly based on fact.

GHOST FILE
Subject   Flying Dutchman
Date   1676
Sighting   Indian Ocean
Status   UNEXPLAINED

WILD STORIES

The real-life *Flying Dutchman* was a seventeenth-century sailing ship owned by a captain named Van der Decken. When the ship vanished in a storm off the coast of South Africa in 1676, many wild stories began to be told about her.

Some said that a dreadful crime had been committed on board. Others said that the crew had been struck down with **plague**. Many believed that the ship was **cursed** because the captain had made a pact with the Devil.

 This famous painting by William Wyllie shows sailors abandoning ship after meeting the ghostly *Flying Dutchman* on the high seas.

MYSTERY SHIP

In 1880, the future King George V of England was sailing to Sydney, Australia, on board the Royal Navy vessel, the HMS Bacchante. At 4 AM one day, the lookout spotted a glowing red sailing ship on the horizon. Mysteriously, as the ghostly ship drew nearer, it suddenly vanished into thin air.

 George V always had a love of the sea and served in the Royal Navy before becoming king of England in 1910.

FACT OR FANTASY?

Tales of ghost ships are not uncommon. According to local folklore, the Caleuche is a ghost ship which sails the seas at night around Chiloé Island, off the coast of Chile. Witnesses speak of hearing music and laughter from on board, before the beautiful ship once again disappears into the night.

WHAT HAPPENED NEXT?

Later that day, a terrible accident took place on board. The seaman who had spotted the mystery ship fell from the rigging and was found lying dead on the forecastle deck.

After this, the future King firmly believed the ghost ship seen that day was the Flying Dutchman. Could it be true?

When did the *Flying Dutchman* disappear?

Who was the captain of the *Flying Dutchman*?

Which British king claimed to have seen the *Flying Dutchman*?

THE GHOST GIRL OF CUCUTA

Occasionally, people invent ghosts to try to fool others. But few invented ghosts have fooled as many people as the ghost girl of Cucuta!

THE GIRL IN WHITE

In May 2007, the Colombian television station RCN showed a film about a ghost that was said to haunt the town of Cucuta in northeast Colombia. The ghost was of a 12-year-old girl who had been murdered in a local park 30 years before. The film included interviews with eyewitnesses, and even video clips showing a sinister white figure gliding through the park at night.

When the film was screened, it caused a sensation. Soon viewers started calling in to say that they had seen the ghost, too!

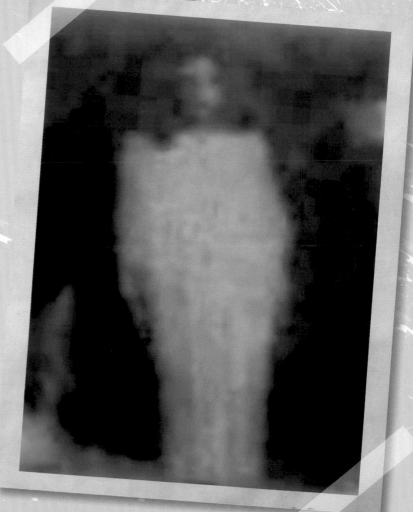

GHOST FILE
Subject   "Ghost girl of Cucuta"
Date   May 2007
Sighting   Villa Camila Park, Cucuta, Colombia
Status   HOAX

 This shot of a ghostly white figure was said to have been taken in Villa Camila Park in Cucuta.

FACT OR FANTASY?

The Cucuta "ghost girl" hoax depended on clever visual effects and camera tricks, but also on convincing performances by the "witnesses." Interviews with people who claimed to have seen the ghost—including a local priest—all made the story seem more believable.

 Interviews with witnesses made the 'ghost girl' story seem very convincing.

WHAT HAPPENED NEXT?

A year later, the Colombian website trikinhuelas.com revealed the truth. The "ghost" was a hoax created by a television news team. The interviews with "witnesses" were faked. The "ghost" shown in the film was a projection of a photograph of a girl taken at a fiesta in 2005.

Which TV channel showed the film of the "ghost?"

In which park was the "ghost" seen?

Which website revealed the hoax?

 This clip of the ghost gliding through the park at night looks very realistic. Would you have been fooled?

THE BELL WITCH

During the early 1800s, the "Bell Witch" was the most famous ghost in the USA. The story of how the vengeful spirit of an old woman terrorized a Tennessee farmer and his family is among the most chilling tales of the supernatural ever told.

This picture of Betsy Bell in the grip of the poltergeist comes from one of the many books about the Bell Witch legend.

GHOST FILE

Subject	The Bell Witch
Date	1817–1820
Sighting	The Bell Farm, Tennessee, USA
Status	UNEXPLAINED

AN UNSEEN FORCE

The haunting began in 1817, when John Bell first noticed strange-looking animals around his farm. Soon afterwards, the family began to hear violent knocking, bumping, and gnawing sounds around the house. At the same time, Betsy, the Bells' young daughter, found herself set upon by a terrifying invisible force, which pulled her hair, scratched, pinched, and even beat her.

SUDDEN DEATH

Soon the unseen force found a voice. Claiming to be an evil witch, it threw objects at members of the family. Then it started to aim its attacks at Betsy's father, John.

On December 20, 1820, three years after the haunting began, John Bell suddenly died. A bottle of poison was found in his bedroom. The witch proudly boasted that she had caused his death.

WHAT HAPPENED NEXT?

About two months later, the haunting ceased. Since that time, many books have been written about the Bell family poltergeist. The story of the Bell Witch is still taught in Tennessee schools today.

Many rural areas of Tennessee have changed little since the days of the Bell Witch. These deserted farm buildings are on the Cumberland plateau, east of Robertson County where the haunting took place.

FACT OR FANTASY?

When the Bell ghost began to speak, it claimed to be the "witch of old Kate Batts," a respectable elderly neighbour of the Bells who lived nearby. However, Kate Batts had no grudge against the Bell family, and John Bell never believed the story. The ghost made many other claims, all equally false.

Where was John Bell's farm?

When did the haunting begin?

Who were the main victims of the haunting?

When Sigmund Adam interviewed Anne-Marie Schneider for a job with his law firm in southern Germany in 1967, there seemed nothing unusual about her. But soon after she started work, Adam noticed a number of very odd things going on in the office...

GHOST FILE

Subject	The Rosenheim Poltergeist
Date	1967
Sighting	Rosenheim, Germany
Status	UNEXPLAINED

SILENT CALLS

First, there were the "silent calls," when the phones would ring and nobody would be on the line. Then the lights started to flicker on and off. Calendars flew off the wall. Drawers shot out from desks. An oak chest slid across the floor of its own accord.

News of the strange events in Rosenheim soon spread. Police went to investigate, and scientists visited the office with tape recorders and cameras. But it was not until a paranormal investigator went to Rosenheim that a pattern began to emerge.

 Anne-Marie Schneider was 19 years old when she went to work in Sigmund Adam's law firm in Rosenheim.

PARANORMAL ACTIVITY

The investigator noticed that the **paranormal** activity occurred only when Anne-Marie Schneider was working in the office—and stopped as soon as she left the building. Interviewing her, the investigator soon found that she was an unhappy young woman, who hated her job and her boss.

FACT OR FANTASY?

The case of the Rosenheim Poltergeist still divides the experts. None of the extreme events that were said to have taken place was ever captured on film. But several scientists were convinced that what they saw was genuine—and there was no obvious sign of evidence being faked.

 Sigmund Adam displays a phone bill he received at the time of the haunting. It shows that he was charged for 600 calls to the **Speaking Clock** —even though all the phones in the office were out of use at the time.

THE SPIRIT DEPARTS

Soon afterwards, Anne-Marie left—and the poltergeist left with her. But nobody could explain how a 19-year-old woman could have triggered such a storm of paranormal activity. Years later, the Rosenheim case remains one of the most bizarre and frightening of recent times.

When did the haunting begin?

How old was Anne-Marie Schneider at the time?

How did scientists try to observe the ghost?

THE KOLKATA POLTERGEIST

In December 2008, a young girl living in Kolkata, India, experienced a terrifying haunting. It started without warning—and ended as mysteriously as it began.

During the haunting, life in the family home was turned upside down and Rima found it impossible to concentrate on her studies.

HAVOC

The Kolkata haunting took place in the house of a man called Ratan Das, just when his eldest daughter, Rima, was about to sit an important school exam.

From December 14 to 27, the poltergeist caused **havoc** in the household. Objects were moved or hidden. Members of the family were pushed and prodded by unseen forces. School books were moved, hidden, and thrown about the room. In desperation, Rima's father called the police. They were as baffled as everyone else.

A MYSTERY UNSOLVED

In the end no one could really explain what had happened. Was the family house triggering the paranormal activity? If so, why was the poltergeist only active when Rima was present?

Could it be that the haunting was simply linked with Rima's fears and worries about her coming exam?

DIARY OF A HAUNTING

December 14 – A vase of flowers is moved.

December 17 – Rima is pushed by invisible hands and her books are thrown around.

December 18 – One of Rima's books bursts into flames.

December 20 – Rima's bed catches fire.

December 21 – Ratan Das calls the police.

December 22 – Rima's bed and books are thrown down the stairs.

December 27 – The haunting ends.

FACT OR FANTASY?

The Kolkata case centered around a young girl who was worried and anxious. Significantly, the attacks were often directed at the books that she was studying. On one occasion, a book she was reading even burst into flames.

GHOST FILE

Subject   The Kolkata Poltergeist
Date   December 2008
Sighting   Kolkata, India
Status   UNEXPLAINED

Where did the haunting take place?

How long did the haunting last?

Who was the main target of the poltergeist?

McCONNELL'S GHOST

Some people claim that paranormal events can be triggered when a person is in extreme danger or **distress**. Could this explain the **baffling** case of McConnell's ghost?

A DATE WITH DEATH

On the morning of December 7, 1918, Lieutenant David McConnell, an 18-year-old British pilot based at Scampton in Lincolnshire, UK, received orders to fly a small two-seater plane to an airfield in Tadcaster 62 miles (100 kilometers) away, returning that same afternoon.

At 11:30 AM, McConnell said goodbye to his roommate and set off for Tadcaster. He never returned. At Tadcaster airfield, his plane crashed on landing and he was killed instantly. His wristwatch, which had been broken at the instant of the crash, read 3:25 PM.

GHOST FILE
Subject   Lieutenant David McConnell
Date   December 7, 1918
Sighting   Scampton Airfield, Lincolnshire, UK
Status   UNEXPLAINED

 First World War fighter planes were very dangerous compared to modern planes. Accidents were frequent – and often fatal.

A FAMILIAR VOICE

At the moment the plane crashed at Tadcaster, McConnell's roommate Larkin was relaxing back at base. Hearing a familiar voice, he looked up and saw the figure of McConnell standing just a few feet away.

"Hello! Back already?"

"Yes," said the figure.

"Got there all right? Had a good trip?"

"Fine, thanks. Well, cheerio!" said the figure, and left.

WHAT HAPPENED NEXT?

When Larkin was told that McConnell had died in a crash that afternoon, he was stunned. If McConnell had died at 3:25 PM in Tadcaster, how could Larkin have spoken to him at exactly that time in Scampton? Had he been dreaming?

Paranormal investigators who studied the case ruled out the possibility of hoax. The mystery of David McConnell's ghost remains unexplained to this day.

FACT OR FANTASY?

A case very similar to McConnell's was reported just the year before. On March 19, 1917, a British pilot was shot down and killed over France. At the exact time of his death, he appeared to both his niece in England and to his half-sister in India.

At what time did McConnell's aircraft crash?

Who saw McConnell's apparition?

What did Larkin say to the apparition?

First World War pilots faced huge risks and were often very **superstitious**. But McConnell's friend Larkin was a reliable witness and had no obvious reason to make up his story.

THE HELPFUL HELMSMAN

In classic tales of the supernatural, ghosts and phantoms are often evil and threatening. But there are times when a supernatural presence can be a life-saver.

TROUBLE AHEAD

In July 1895, the lone yachtsman Joshua Slocum was on board his boat, Spray, somewhere off the coast of West Africa. Slocum was on his way to becoming the first man ever to sail round the world single-handed. But right now he was in trouble. After setting out from the Azores in the mid-Atlantic, he had run into fierce storms—and now he was sick with severe stomach cramps.

Joshua Slocum (1844–1909) was a Canadian-American seaman and a well-known writer. His book *Alone Around the World* is a classic story of seafaring adventure.

GHOST FILE

Subject: Ghost of fifteenth-century sailor
Sighting: North Atlantic Ocean
Date: 27 July 1895
Status: UNEXPLAINED

THE GHOST PILOT

Abandoning the helm, Slocum crawled off to get some rest, and was soon asleep. After some time below, he was getting ready to go back on deck when he was astonished to see a tall figure at the helm, dressed in the clothes of a fifteenth-century sailor.

Joshua Slocum's sailing boat Spray, photographed in 1898.

FACT OR FANTASY?

Most people would say that Slocum simply imagined that he saw a ghostly sailor. Columbus was already in Slocum's thoughts, as he had read about Columbus's travels before setting out. But this does not explain how the ship stayed on course during the night.

"Señor," the **helmsman** said, "I mean you no harm. I am one of Columbus' crew, the pilot of the Pinta, come to aid you. Lie quiet and I will guide your ship tonight."

Slocum did as he was told. The next day when he woke, he found that the boat was exactly on course. He later wrote, "Columbus himself could not have held her more exactly on course. I had been in the presence of a friend and a seaman of great experience."

Where was Slocum's boat when the incident took place?

What was wrong with Slocum at the time?

Who did the ghostly sailor claim to be?

ANCIENT MYSTERIES

PUZZLES FROM THE PAST

This chapter is all about ancient mysteries. Some have baffled the experts for centuries. A few have been solved, but most have not. Read the evidence and see if you can come up with explanations of your own.

HISTORY OR MYSTERY?

Sometimes a mystery is caused by a simple lack of evidence. Some people think that King Arthur is a fairy story, but others believe that Arthur was a real person who ruled Britain in about the year 500 CE. Unfortunately, in the years that followed the fall of the Roman Empire, nearly all the records of what happened in Britain at that time were lost. The result is that we have no way of knowing if Arthur really existed or not.

 Glastonbury in the English county of Somerset is believed to be the place where King Arthur and Queen Guinevere were buried.

Stories about King Arthur are known the world over—but did Arthur really exist?

FACTS AND THEORIES

Other ancient mysteries have lasted because so many possible answers could fit the facts. For example, we know that the **pyramids** were built as **tombs** for the **pharaohs** of ancient Egypt. But nobody knows how such huge buildings could have been built by men using only stone and copper tools. **Historians** have plenty of ideas, but no one really knows which theory is right.

 The discovery of how to read hieroglyphs has allowed us to find out a huge amount about the ancient Egyptians.

DECODING THE PAST

A few ancient mysteries have been solved with the help of new evidence. For centuries, people knew that Egyptian **hieroglyphs** were a type of writing, but nobody could read them. Then a stone was discovered that had the same messages carved on It in ancient Greek, demotic, and in hieroglyphs. Because experts could understand ancient Greek, they were able to puzzle out the hieroglyphs. Today, historians can read ancient Egyptian writings easily.

 Wo now know that these giant pyramids were built as burial sites for the Egyptian pharaohs.

The mystery of Stonehenge has fascinated people for centuries. This great stone circle is one of the world's most important **prehistoric** sites. But how were the giant stones put in place? Who built it—and why?

MYSTERY FILE

Name Stonehenge
Date 3100 – 1700 BCE
Place Wiltshire, England
Status UNEXPLAINED

Some of the giant stones that form Stonehenge weigh up to 25 tons each. About half were dragged from the Welsh mountains, more than 200 miles (320 kilometers) away.

WHAT IS A HENGE?

A **henge** is a mysterious type of prehistoric monument found in western Europe. It consists of a large round ditch dug into the ground with a bank of earth around it. Most henges have upright stones or wooden posts arranged inside them. Nobody knows what the henges were for, but they would have taken hundreds of people many months to build, so they must have been very important.

A diagram of Stonehenge showing the stone circles and the bank and ditch surrounding the site.

FACTS AND THEORIES

Some think Stonehenge was a temple where people worshipped the sun or the moon. Others think it was a calendar that allowed the people to tell what time of year it was. One recent idea is that it was a place where important local rulers were buried.

STONEHENGE TIMELINE

3100 BCE — Henge earthworks dug.

3000 BCE — Wooden posts erected within the henge.

2600 BCE — "Bluestones" erected.

2400 BCE — Bluestones removed. Huge "Sarsen" stones erected within the henge.

2100 BCE — Bluestones returned.

1600 BCE — Stonehenge abandoned.

WHO BUILT STONEHENGE?

For centuries, people thought that giants or **demons** had built Stonehenge. Then, starting in 1919, **archeologists** began to **excavate** the area around it.

At certain times of the year, the stones line up with the sun and moon. For instance, the midsummer sun rises over the "Heelstone," while at midwinter the tallest stone lines up with the moon. There are several burial sites in or near Stonehenge. There are also other mounds, ditches, and henges in the area. Although archeologists have excavated most of these remains, nobody can explain what purpose they served or why they were built.

 People who follow ancient religions such as **druidism** still gather at Stonehenge every year to worship nature and celebrate the seasons.

What is a henge?

When were the earthworks first dug?

When was the surrounding area first excavated?

Who were the first Native Americans and where did they come from? Until recently, it was thought they came from Asia via a narrow land bridge with Siberia, but now experts are not so sure.

STONE WEAPONS

Among the earliest known inhabitants of the Americas were the Clovis people. The Clovis were **hunter-gatherers** who lived in North America about 13,000 years ago.

The Clovis people used an unusual type of stone weapon known as the Clovis point, which has a flattened oval shape. These are very like weapons that have been found in Europe.

Recently, scientists have found that **the genes** of Native American peoples are very like those of Europeans. This could mean that some of their ancestors originally came to America from Europe, rather than from Asia.

Clovis points were first discovered in the city of Clovis, New Mexico. They have since been found throughout North America and as far south as Venezuela.

MYSTERY FILE
Name Clovis People
Date c.13,000 BCE
Place North America
Status UNEXPLAINED

COINCIDENCE?

Because Clovis points are so like stone tools found in Europe, some experts believe that the Clovis people originally came from Europe. It is thought they could have traveled to America via an ice-shelf that once joined the continents.

However, the stone weapons found in Europe stopped being made a thousand years before the time of the Clovis people. Perhaps the similarities between the two are just a coincidence. Nobody knows.

Inuit hunters in the Arctic live by catching fish and hunting animals. If the Clovis people moved westward across the Arctic ice, they may have survived in much the same way.

FACTS AND THEORIES

Climate scientists have discovered that around 15,000 BCE, Arctic sea ice formed a vast land mass stretching as far south as France. This would have made it possible for European people to move westward, living on fish and Arctic animals much like modern Inuit peoples.

When did the Clovis people live in North America?

What is a Clovis point?

How might the Clovis people have reached the Americas?

In recent years, we have found out more and more about the amazing wonders of ancient Egypt. But before experts learned to read Egyptian writing, much of what we know today was surrounded in mystery.

SACRED WRITING

When archeologists first began to study Egyptian temples and tombs, they found that they were covered with carvings of animals, people, objects, and strange symbols. They knew from ancient Roman writings that the carvings meant something—but what?

The Egyptian symbols carved on this tablet are known as hieroglyphs. The word "hieroglyph" means literally "sacred carving."

In the third millennium BCE, the great Step Pyramid of Dhoser was part of a huge civilization on the banks of the River Nile.

MYSTERY FILE

Name	Egyptian hieroglyphic writing
Date	330 BCE – 393 CE
Place	Egypt
Status	SOLVED

FACTS AND THEORIES

In 1824, a French **linguist** and historian, Jean-Francois Champollion, solved the riddle of the Rosetta Stone. He noticed that certain symbols were enclosed in an oval shape called a **cartouche**. These were names, while the other symbols stood for words, sounds, or ideas.

THE ROSETTA STONE

In 1799, French soldiers in Egypt found a tablet known as the Rosetta Stone. On it, the same message was carved in Greek, hieroglyphs and demotic (another type of Egyptian writing). Because experts could read the Greek and demotic, they were able to work out what the hieroglyphs meant.

The Rosetta Stone dates back to around 196 BCE. Its discovery and later decoding allowed experts to make the first breakthroughs in understanding Egyptian hieroglyphs.

WHAT HAPPENED NEXT?

Since then, thousands of Egyptian texts and carvings have been deciphered, or worked out. These have revealed the entire history of Egypt from about 3200 BCE to 300 BCE. The names of rulers, priests, princesses and workers have been revealed. We know how Egyptians lived and what they did. The mystery was solved at last.

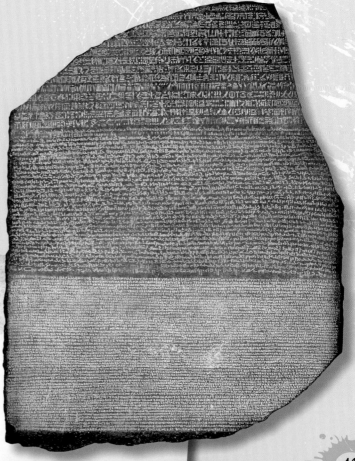

What is Egyptian writing called?

Who discovered the Rosetta Stone?

Who first decoded the Rosetta Stone?

THE LOST WORLD OF THE MINOANS

From around 2700 to 1450 BCE, Minoan people built a great civilization on the Greek island of Crete. Some of their palaces and temples have survived and are studied by experts. But the greatest Minoan mystery of all is still unsolved...

 The carvings on this Minoan clay tablet represent the first written language in Europe.

CLAY TABLETS

In 1900, the archeologist Arthur Evans discovered more than 2,000 clay tablets covered with mysterious **symbols** on the site of the Minoan palace at Knossos in Crete. In ancient times, the tablets would have been left in the sun to dry. Luckily, some were in buildings that had been destroyed in a fire. The fire had hardened the tablets, and so the tablets had survived down the ages.

The tablets showed that the Minoans had created a written language—the first in Europe. But what did it mean?

 The palace and temple at Knossos were the centre of a civilization that once stretched right across the Aegean.

MYSTERY FILE

Name   "Linear A" script
Date   2100–1650 BCE
Place   Crete
Status UNEXPLAINED

MYSTERY SCRIPT

Evans worked out that the inscriptions were in three different languages: a hieroglyphic script, and two other scripts, which he called simply "Linear A" and "Linear B." When "Linear B" was **deciphered** in 1952, the tablets revealed a lot about the Myceneans, who conquered the Minoans around 1400 BCE.

The Minoans were skilled artists and craftsmen, and Minoan vases and jewellery are among the great treasures of the ancient world.

"Linear A" clearly belonged to a different, earlier language—and since nobody knows what language the Minoans spoke, all attempts to decipher the "Linear A" texts have failed.

FACTS AND THEORIES

In 1952, a young Englishman, Michael Ventris, became the first to decipher the tablets found at Knossos on Crete. Ventris discovered that the "Linear B" language was a form of ancient Greek, but the language of "Linear A" is unknown. It may be Iranian, or a type of Phoenician or Greek.

Where was the centre of Minoan civilization?

When were the Minoan clay tablets discovered?

What names did Arthur Evans give to the two Minoan scripts?

The story of the lost world of Atlantis has fascinated people for centuries. Some believe Atlantis was the site of a very advanced civilization. But could a whole continent and its people *really* disappear beneath the waves?

WHERE WAS ATLANTIS?

The earliest descriptions of Atlantis were by ancient Greek writers, who claimed to have been told all about it by Egyptian priests. According to legend, it was a highly advanced island kingdom, where the people were able to build machines and ships. But if Atlantis really existed, where was the evidence?

MYSTERY FILE

Name	Atlantis
Date	c.9600 BCE
Place	Unknown
Status	UNEXPLAINED

This ruined temple is on the Mediterranean island of Thera, one of many places where Atlantis is thought to have been located.

FACTS AND THEORIES

*Recent research into the **eruption** at Thera has shown that it was powerful and highly destructive. Volcanic ash would have plunged much of the Mediterranean into darkness, and the tidal wave that followed would have caused huge damage. Perhaps a disaster this big could have swept away an entire kingdom.*

THE SEARCH FOR CLUES

Some people thought that the Azores in the north Atlantic were the remains of Atlantis. Others preferred Cuba, the Bahamas or the Canaries. By 1900, historians realized that the ancient stories could not be relied on, so they went back to the original evidence to look for clues.

One of the most detailed descriptions of Atlantis was by the Greek philosopher Plato (c.427–c.348 BCE).

WHAT HAPPENED NEXT?

During the 1950s, archeologists discovered that around 1550 BCE, the Mediterranean island of Thera had suffered a massive volcanic eruption. An entire city had been destroyed, along with towns on nearby islands. If Atlantis had been destroyed 900 years before the time of the Greeks, instead of 9000 years, then the story might fit!

Who first told Greek writers about Atlantis?

Which island was devastated in about 1550 BCE?

Who wrote a detailed account of Atlantis?

CITY OF GOLD

When Spanish people first conquered the Americas in the sixteenth century, many believed there was a city called Eldorado, or the "golden one," waiting to be discovered. But finding it wasn't easy!

MYSTERY FILE
Name Eldorado
Date c.1520-1940
Place South or North America
Status SOLVED

Led by the soldier and explorer Hernán Cortés, Spanish forces were eager to get their hands on the riches of the Aztec empire of Mexico.

The historic city of Machu Picchu is the best preserved of all the Inca cities and is now a major tourist attraction.

STOLEN GOLD

In 1519, a small force of Spanish soldiers led by Hernán Cortés (1485–1547) accidentally discovered the Aztec empire of Mexico. The Spanish used their modern guns, steel weapons, and armor to conquer the Aztec Indians who lived there. Cortés and his men became very rich on stolen Aztec gold.

INCA TREASURE

In 1532, Francisco Pizarro (c.1471–1541) conquered the even richer Inca empire of South America and stole huge amounts of gold from its people. Spanish explorers began asking about gold wherever they went. Local people told them about a great city filled with gold some distance away. Some said it was to the east, others to the north or south. For years the Spanish searched, but never found it.

 Gold was a sacred metal to the Incas and was often used to create beautiful jewellery like this ancient headdress.

FACTS AND THEORIES

Apart from the kingdoms of the Aztecs and Incas, we now know that there was no "golden city" anywhere in the Americas. The most likely explanation is that local people spread rumors about Eldorado in the hope that the Spanish would go away and leave them in peace.

WHAT HAPPENED NEXT?

Later, others took up the challenge. In 1595, the English explorer Sir Walter Raleigh traveled up the Orinoco River in search of a rich city. The Orinoco was explored in 1804, but no city was discovered. In the 1920s, the British adventurer Percy Fawcett set off in search of a lost ancient city in the Amazon rainforest. Neither he, nor the city, were ever found.

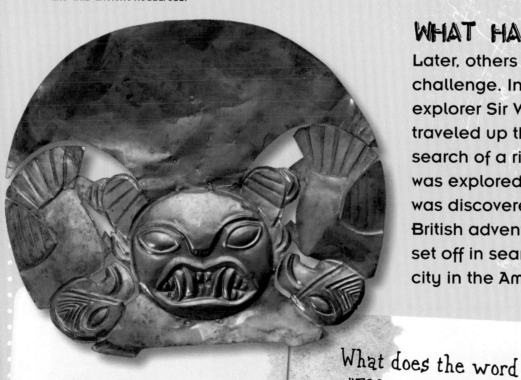

Who traveled up the Orinoco River in search of a rich city?

What does the word "Eldorado" mean?

Who led the army that conquered the Aztec Empire?

ISLAND OF STONES

In the Pacific Ocean, thousands of miles from the nearest civilization, lies Easter Island. This strange and mysterious place is famous for its **monumental** stone statues, known as "moai."

A THRIVING COMMUNITY

When Dutch explorer Jacob Roggeveen (1659–1729) first discovered Easter Island in 1722, he found a **thriving** community of more than 3,000 people. Yet when a British ship arrived in 1825, her captain, James Cook, found a very different picture: statues had been knocked over and damaged, and many of the island's inhabitants had left, never to return. By 1877, only 111 remained.

"Moai" are huge human figures carved from rock that stare from the hillsides of Easter island. The tallest are almost 30 feet (10 meters) high and weigh around 75 tons.

MYSTERY FILE

Name	Easter Island
Date	1860s
Place	Pacific Ocean
Mystery	SOLVED

MYSTERY COLLAPSE

The mystery of what had happened to the people puzzled historians. How could the community on Easter Island have collapsed, apparently within just 40 years?

WHAT HAPPENED NEXT?

In 1888, when Easter Island was taken over by Chile, historians began to study it to find out what had happened.

Eventually, several answers were found. Too many trees had been cut down, leaving the land exposed to the **elements**. Fighting between different tribes and a massive raid by Peruvian **slave-traders** had also reduced the population.

Arriving at Easter Island in 1825, Captain James Cook found the people hungry and the landscape bleak and bare-looking.

THE ISLAND TODAY

Today, the islanders number just a few hundred. But they still keep alive their traditions and fight to protect the ancient "moai" from further destruction.

FACTS AND THEORIES

*Easter Island was once covered in forests, but in 1600 the last tree was chopped down, and lack of timber soon meant there were no boats left for fishing. The lack of trees also meant that wind and rain removed the topsoil. Crops failed, people went hungry and **disputes** broke out.*

Which Dutch explorer first discovered Easter Island?

Who visited the island in 1825?

How many islanders were left in 1877?

THE LEGEND OF LYONESSE

According to legend, a large and fertile land once stretched from Cornwall in the UK to the Isles of Scilly—until disaster came to Lyonesse one night...

A LAND OF PLENTY

The oldest stories about Lyonesse say that it was a rich farming area that belonged to the King of Cornwall during the time of King Arthur. The land was below sea level, but was protected by a high bank called a dyke. The gates in the dyke were opened at low tide to allow water out, but closed at high tide to stop the water rushing in.

One night, the man who was supposed to watch the dyke gates decided to go out and enjoy himself with his friends instead. The tide came in, gushed through the open gates and flooded Lyonesse. After the disaster, Cornwall was so poor that it was easily overrun by the English.

MYSTERY FILE

Name The Lost Land of Lyonesse
Date c.650
Place Under the sea between the Atlantic Ocean and the English Channel
Status DISPROVED

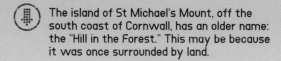

The island of St Michael's Mount, off the south coast of Cornwall, has an older name: the "Hill in the Forest." This may be because it was once surrounded by land.

DID LYONESSE EXIST?

In the sixteenth century, Cornish people still referred to the Seven Stones reef off Land's End as the "City of Lions" (Lyonesse). It was also said that you could hear the bells of the drowned city ringing during stormy weather.

 The knight Tristram of Lyonesse was a famous hero of Cornish legend.

FACTS AND THEORIES

Recent maps of the seabed show that most of the area between Cornwall and the Isles of Scilly is too deep to have been a tidal land. It seems doubtful that Lyonesse ever existed. Perhaps the tales of Lyonesse recall the time before the sea levels rose, 1500 years ago.

At very low tides, stone walls and ruined houses can be seen on the seabed off the Isles of Scilly. It is also possible to see the remains of field walls along the sands between Tresco and Sampson. Roman records state that the Isles of Scilly were one much larger island in those days. This area flooded some time between 400 and 1100 CE. Perhaps this large island was the original Lyonesse.

 The King of Cornwall once ruled his kingdom from the site of this ruined castle at Tintagel on the north coast of Cornwall.

Where was the land of Lyonesse?

Who ruled the land?

Which island has another name meaning "the hill in the forest"?

The mighty pyramids of Egypt are among the most impressive monuments of all time. For centuries, people have been trying to puzzle out how they were built without the use of modern tools.

MYSTERY FILE

Name	Egyptian Pyramids
Date	c.2650–c.1800 BCE
Place	Egypt
Status	UNEXPLAINED

THE GREAT PYRAMID

Of the 138 pyramids in Egypt, the biggest is the Great Pyramid of Giza. It was originally 480 feet (147 meters) tall and 755 feet (231 meters) along each side. Nearly 6.1 million tons (6 million tonnes) of stone were needed to build it. Most of its stones weigh about 2 tons each, but some are up to 91 tons (90 tonnes) in weight.

 This carved statue is of the Pharaoh Khufu who ordered the Great Pyramid to be built in c.2571 BCE.

The Great Pyramid is the oldest and largest of the three pyramids at Giza in Egypt. For centuries, it was the tallest building in the world.

FACTS AND THEORIES

*By studying hieroglyphs, experts have learned that the pyramids were tombs of the pharaohs, or rulers, of ancient Egypt. Inside each is a **network** of tunnels and chambers. The pharaoh and his family were buried in the chambers along with furniture, clothes, jewels and food for use in the next life.*

SKILL AND CARE

The pyramid's sheer size is amazing, but so is the skill of the Egyptian builders. The base slopes by just over half an inch (15 millimeters), and the sides vary by only 2 1/4 inches (58 millimeters). Originally, it was covered with a layer of polished white limestone.

Other pyramids are not so large, but they are just as impressive. It is thought that the pyramid shape was chosen to copy the rays of the Sun striking the Earth.

This is one of the giant stones that once covered the outer face of the pyramid.

STONE ON STONE

Nobody is certain how the pyramids were built. Most people think that the stone blocks were carved in a quarry, dragged on sleds, and then hauled into position up a ramp of sand. If so, each pyramid would have taken up to 30,000 men 20 years to build. But no trace of ramps has ever been found.

Another theory is that the stones were dragged up a stone ramp inside the pyramid, but again, no ramp has been found.

King's burial chamber

Queen's burial chamber

Grand Gallery

Entrance

The diagram shows the inside of the Great Pyramid, including the upward-sloping Grand Gallery to the king's burial chamber and the lower route to the queen's.

When was the Great Pyramid built?

What were the pyramids used for?

What was the shape of the pyramids said to copy?

THE LEGEND OF TROY

According to Greek legend, in about 1250 BCE an army from Greece attacked the city of Troy and destroyed it after a long **siege**. But how much of the legend was based on fact?

STORIES AND POEMS

In ancient times, many stories were told about the Trojan War. The most famous was the **epic** poem the *Iliad*, composed by the Greek poet Homer in about 850 BCE. The Greeks believed that there had been a real Trojan War, though some of Homer's stories were clearly made up.

This golden mask was found at Mycenae by Heinrich Schliemann in 1876. It dates to about the time of the Trojan War and was placed over the face of a king of Mycenae when he was buried.

These remains of the city of Troy are at Hisarlik in modern Turkey.

HISTORY OR MYTH?

By the nineteenth century, people thought that the Trojan War was just a **myth**. Then, in 1870, the German archaeologist Heinrich Schliemann (1822–1890) collected all the clues about Troy and began to dig at a place called Hisarlik in Turkey. What Schliemann discovered showed that Troy could have been a real city after all.

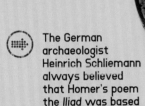

The German archaeologist Heinrich Schliemann always believed that Homer's poem the *Iliad* was based on real events.

FACTS AND THEORIES

Recent research confirms that Troy was a real city. In the 1990s, documents were found that refer to a war between "Taruisa" and Greece. Most experts now agree that "Taruisa"/Hisarlik is Troy, and that the Trojan War was an actual historical event.

MYSTERY FILE

Name	Troy (Illium)
Date	c.1250 BCE
Place	North-western Turkey
Status	UNSOLVED

CLUES AMONG THE RUINS

The ruins found by Schliemann showed that the site had been inhabited from about 3000 BCE to about 500 CE. Schliemann found one layer of buildings that had been destroyed by fire. This may have been the city destroyed during the Trojan War, but not everyone is convinced. The built-up area seems to have been too small to be a major city and the defences had curious gaps. Much more work needs to be done at Hisarlik before we have the answers.

When was the Trojan War fought?

Who wrote an epic poem about the Trojan War?

Who first excavated Hisarlik and identified it as Troy?

HERO OF CAMELOT

Over the centuries, many tales have been told about King Arthur of Britain. He is said to have been a worthy knight who ruled over a golden age of peace and plenty. True or not, the stories have certainly stood the test of time.

The young Arthur tries on the crown of Britain. At his side is the magic sword Excalibur.

MYSTERY FILE

Name	King Arthur
Date	c.500 CE
Place	Britain
Status	UNEXPLAINED

KNIGHTS OF CAMELOT

According to legend, King Arthur ruled Britain from Camelot. He led his famous Knights of the Round Table on a series of adventures, including the search for the Holy Grail, the sacred cup used by Jesus at the Last Supper.

At some point, Arthur's nephew Mordred is said to have grown jealous of his power and begun a civil war. This ended in the death of both men at the Battle of Camlann. After Arthur's death, Britain was plunged into a dark period of war and disaster.

FACTS AND THEORIES

Most of the stories about Arthur that we know today come from a book called Le Morte d'Arthur written by Sir Thomas Malory (c. 1405–1471). Some historians now think that Arthur really existed, but there is little mention of him in any of the important records of the time.

THE "REAL" ARTHUR?

Around 1150, Geoffrey of Monmouth wrote what is said to be a history of the "real" Arthur. According to Geoffrey, Arthur became ruler of Britain after the Romans left and defeated the invading Saxons at the Battle of Badon Hill, some time between 490 and 517 CE. However, Geoffrey does not say where he got his information. Many think he simply invented it.

This large hill fort known as Cadbury Castle is in the English county of Somerset. Situated close to the river Cam, it is often thought to have been the site of Arthur's court at Camelot.

What was the name of Arthur's castle?

What was the name of Arthur's magic sword?

Who wrote about Arthur in around 1150?

With its famous shore temple, Mahabalipuram is one of the most beautiful historic sites in southern India. But if the legends are true, the monuments that survive today are just **a fragment** of what once existed.

VENGEANCE OF VISHNU

According to an ancient **Hindu** legend, in 550 CE, Hiranyakasipu, the ruler of Mahabalipuram, refused to worship the god Vishnu. His son, Prahlada, wanted to build a temple to Vishnu, and the two argued. Shouting that Vishnu did not exist, the father angrily kicked the shrine that Prahlada had built to Vishnu. Vishnu then appeared and killed Hiranyakasipu.

When Prahlada became ruler, he built seven beautiful **pagodas** that were said to be the finest in all India. The god Indra then became jealous of the fine temples to Vishnu and caused six of them to sink into the sea. The surviving temple is known as the Shore Temple.

The shore temple at Mahabalipuram is believed to be one of seven dedicated to the Hindu god Vishnu.

WHAT HAPPENED NEXT?

For many years, the fishermen of Mahabalipuram claimed to see traces of buildings in the sea. Then in 2004, a giant tidal wave called a tsunami struck, shifting banks of sand that had lain undisturbed for centuries. As the seawater retreated, the ruins of buildings began to appear about 1600 feet (500 meters) from the shore.

Archeologists began digging in the sand and found the ruins of two temples. Under the sea, divers found stone walls and beautiful carvings. Explorations and excavations are still going on to find out if the legendary Seven Pagodas really existed.

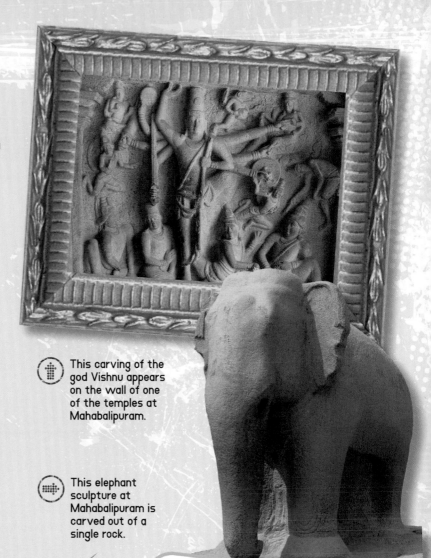

This carving of the god Vishnu appears on the wall of one of the temples at Mahabalipuram.

This elephant sculpture at Mahabalipuram is carved out of a single rock.

MYSTERY FILE
Name The Seven Pagodas
Date c.750 CE
Place Mahabalipuram, India
Status UNEXPLAINED

FACTS AND THEORIES

Recent research has found that an earthquake in about 1300 CE caused the land to slip beneath the sea. The shore temple that still stands has been dated to about 750 CE. Nearby are several other temples, but these are much smaller and less impressive.

To which god were the Seven Pagodas dedicated?

Which god is said to have become jealous?

What is a tsunami?

STRANGE ANIMALS

WHAT IS A CRYPTID?

For centuries, people have told stories of strange, often scary creatures that do not seem to belong to any known **species**. These animals are called **cryptids**, or "hidden ones." But how do we know whether or not a cryptid really exists?

 The Loch Ness monster is one of the most famous cryptids of all time. This picture first appeared in 1934, but was later found to be a fake.

INVESTIGATING CRYPTIDS

Many of the stories about cryptids come from ancient myths and legends. But some people claim to have taken photos and videos of cryptids—and even collected evidence of them, such as footprints, droppings, and fur. Of course, none of this proves that a cryptid really exists. Some of the evidence has been shown to be fake—but not all of it...

 This footprint photographed in 1951 is said to be that of a **Yeti**, a giant ape-like creature believed by some to live in the mountains of Nepal.

CRYPTID HUNTERS

Often the evidence for cryptids is strong. But scientists will not say that a cryptid really exists until it has been captured and studied in a laboratory.

A person who searches for cryptids is called a **cryptozoologist**, which means "a person who studies hidden animals." People who search for cryptids often need to travel to far-off parts of the world. They must know how to survive in jungles, forests, mountains, and other harsh environments.

Cryptids are often confused with animals that belong to known species. This hand skeleton was said to belong to a Yeti, but was later found to be that of a bear.

COLLECTING EVIDENCE

Among the tools used by cryptid hunters are:

Camera	To take photos and movies.
Plaster	To take casts of footprints.
Plastic bags	To collect and store evidence such as hairs, droppings, etc.
Traps	To catch cryptids for future study.
Maps and notebooks	To record the time and place of sightings.

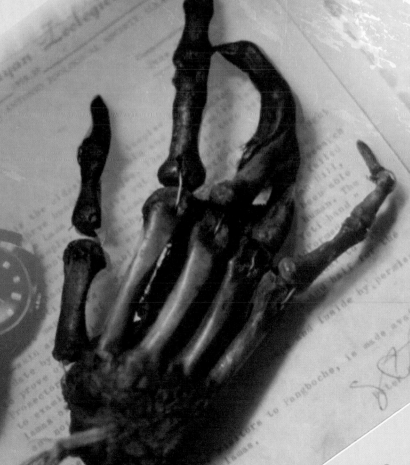

How would you feel if you came across mysterious footprints on a mountainside, or saw a giant creature coming towards you through the snow?

CRYPTID FILE

Subject	Yeti
Height	About 5 feet (1.6 meters)
Habitat	Himalayan mountains
Status	UNEXPLAINED

IN SEARCH OF THE YETI

In the late nineteenth century, travelers to Nepal and Tibet began to hear stories of a huge ape-like creature that lived deep in the Himalayan mountains. Local people called it the "Yeti," or "animal of the rocks." The creature was said to be very strong, but it was shy and usually ran off when it saw humans.

In 1951, Eric Shipton, a well-known British mountaineer, was on a climbing trip in Nepal when he saw strange footprints, which his guide told him were made by the Yeti. Shipton followed the tracks and took photos of them. His pictures were later published all over the world.

Many climbers and local people claim to have seen the **Yeti** hunting for food in the mountains. Some even claim to have captured the creature on film.

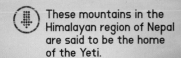

These mountains in the Himalayan region of Nepal are said to be the home of the Yeti.

STRANGE CRIES

One person who claims to have actually seen the Yeti is British mountaineer Don Whillans. During an **expedition** to the Himalayas in 1970, Whillans was looking for a place to pitch his tent when he heard strange cries. Later that night, he saw a large shape moving in the darkness outside. The next day, he found footprints and spent 20 minutes watching through binoculars as a large, ape-like creature searched for food not far from his camp.

This animal **scalp** is believed to belong to a Yeti. It is kept by monks at Kumjung **monastery**, high in the Himalayan mountains.

FACT OR FAKE?

The most recent sighting of Yeti footprints was by US TV presenter Josh Gates in December 2007. Gates found a huge five-toed pawmark 13 inches long and 10 wide (33 x 25 centimeters). Two heelprints were also found. An expert who examined the prints was convinced they were genuine.

How tall is the Yeti believed to be?

Who first took photos of Yeti footprints?

Which climber claims to have seen the Yeti?

If you go down to the woods today... watch out for **Bigfoot!** More than 300 people claim to have seen this fearsome creature in the remote forests of the northwest USA.

THE BIGFOOT TRAIL

In 1958, workmen were building a road in Bluff Creek, a remote part of northern California, when they found mysterious footprints made by a creature that they nicknamed "Bigfoot." The reports made headlines across the USA, and Bigfoot became famous. But could Bigfoot really exist? In 1967, investigators Roger Patterson and Robert Gimlin decided to visit Bluff Creek to find out.

Cryptid hunter Robert Gimlin holds plaster casts made from footprints found at Bluff Creek, California, in 1967.

Dense forest like this still covers vast areas of the American northwest.

What is the Native American name for Bigfoot?

How heavy is Bigfoot said to be?

Who claimed to have filmed Bigfoot in 1967?

 Native Americans often used to tell stories about a powerful ape-like animal that lived in the woods. Could this be the creature they called "Sasquatch?"

CRYPTID FILE

Subject	Bigfoot
Height	7.10 feet (2.4 meters)
Weight	485 pounds (220 kilograms)
Habitat	Northwest USA
Status	UNEXPLAINED

BIGFOOT THE MOVIE

After two weeks of searching, Patterson and Gimlin were riding up a narrow creek when they saw a huge ape-like animal about 80 feet (25 meters) away. Patterson's horse was alarmed and reared up, throwing him from the saddle. Soon Patterson was back on his feet and filmed the creature as it walked away into the woods.

Patterson's film of Bigfoot caused huge debate. Patterson swore on his deathbed that the film was genuine. Gimlin also believes that what the two men saw was the North American Bigfoot.

FACT OR FAKE?

The Patterson film has been examined many times by experts. Some scientists say that there is no such thing as Bigfoot and that the "creature" in the film is just a man in an ape-suit. Others claim it would be impossible for an actor to fake the muscle movements that the creature makes in the film.

BEWARE THE BUNYIP!

Before the first European settlers arrived in Australia in 1788, "Terra Australis" was thought to be full of bizarre and terrifying creatures—and none was more frightening than the **Bunyip!**

FEROCIOUS

The first reports of the Bunyip came from **Aboriginal** tribesmen. They warned settlers to watch out for a **ferocious** seal-like creature about 30 feet (9 meters) long that lived in lakes and lagoons and attacked anyone who came near.

CRYPTID FILE

Subject Bunyip
Size About 30 feet (9 meters) long
Habitat Southeast Australia
Status EXPLAINED!

Some experts believe that Bunyips were really giant **marsupials** known as diprotodons. Diprotodons lived about 1.6 million years ago. Their bones have been found in many places across Australia.

STRANGE SOUNDS

Between 1840 and 1850, several settlers reported seeing strange **amphibious** creatures. Unusual bones were found buried in the mud of lakes and rivers. Suddenly, people all over the country were talking about Bunyips. Many claimed to have heard strange sounds coming from the lagoons at night.

According to one theory, the Bunyip was a type of seal that had strayed far from the coast and had gradually **adapted** to life in rivers and lagoons..

FACT OR FAKE?

In 1846, a skull believed to be that of a Bunyip was found on the banks of the Murrumbidgee River in New South Wales and put on display in a museum in Sydney. However, a scientist who examined it decided that it belonged to a deformed foal, and was not evidence of a new species.

WHAT HAPPENED NEXT?

By the 1880s, experts began to realize that the old stories told by the Aborigines were about a mythical beast, not a real creature. Some of the bones found in old lakes were identified as belonging to a prehistoric giant **wombat** called the diprotodon. Real Bunyips probably never existed—but stories about them are still part of Australian folklore to this day.

How did the first settlers hear about the Bunyip?

Where were Bunyips believed to live?

Where was the skull of a Bunyip said to have been found in 1846?

SEA MONSTER AHOY!

Ever since ships have sailed the seas, sailors have been spinning tales about fantastic sea creatures. Most are probably untrue, or at least exaggerated. But some cannot be explained quite so easily...

TERRIBLE CREATURE

An early recorded sighting of a sea monster was by a Scandinavian missionary, Hans Egede. On July 6, 1734, Egede's ship was sailing past the coast of Greenland when suddenly all on board "saw a most terrible creature, resembling nothing they had ever seen before."

Egede wrote: "The monster lifted its head higher than the crow's nest on the main mast. Giant fins propelled it through the water. Later the sailors saw its tail as well. The monster was longer than our whole ship."

 This scene is imaginary, but the giant squid pictured here is a real creature that is found in many of the world's oceans.

THE DAEDALUS SIGHTING

On August 6, 1848, the British warship HMS *Daedalus* was cruising in the South Atlantic when the duty officer spotted what looked like a giant sea snake in the water. For 20 minutes, everybody on board watched the serpent moving through the sea with its oval-shaped head poking out of the water.

Later, Captain M'Quhae of the *Daedalus* wrote a report of the sighting. Scientists did not believe the story, but the captain insisted that every word was true.

Who saw a sea serpent in 1734?

Where did the sighting take place?

How long was the serpent?

CRYPTID FILE

Subject Sea serpent
Length 65 feet (20 meters)
Sighting In oceans worldwide
Status UNEXPLAINED

FACT OR FAKE?

Because the oceans are so vast, it is possible that large creatures may be living there undetected. In 2003, a US cryptozoologist examined all the evidence for sea cryptids. He suggested that the oceans might contain up to 10 types of large creature that do not belong to any known species.

THE MAPINGUARI

Long ago in the tropical rainforests of Brazil and Bolivia, people told of a **sloth**-like creature with a terrible cry—and an even more terrible smell. Meet the Mapinguari!

Locals describe the Mapinguari as being about 9.8 feet (2.5 meters) tall, covered in red fur, foul-smelling and with claws strong enough to rip apart a fully grown palm tree.

CRYPTID FILE

Subject	Mapinguari
Height	About 9.8 feet (2.5 meters)
Habitat	South America
Status	UNEXPLAINED

CLAWED ANIMAL

In 1888, Ramón Lista, the governor of Santa Cruz Province in Argentina, was out hunting when he suddenly saw a huge clawed animal rearing up on its hind legs in front of him. Terrified, Lista shot at it—but missed. While Lista reloaded his gun, the animal walked away into the scrubland.

THE MYLODON

Later, Lista told his friend, zoologist Florentino Ameghino, about his experience. From his description, Ameghino soon realized that the creature was almost identical to the Mylodon, a type of giant sloth that was thought to have died out centuries before.

Two years later, a "big game" hunter called Vernon Hesketh-Prichard set out for Patagonia to shoot a "Mapinguari" and bring it back for study. Despite travelling for over 900 miles (1500 kilometers) through the forests and grasslands of Patagonia, Hesketh-Prichard eventually gave up his quest and returned empty-handed.

FACT OR FAKE?

Most of the sightings of the Mapinguari took place more than 250 years ago, but many people believe that the creature still exists. The ornithologist David Oren has searched for the Mapinguari for many years. However, none of the evidence he has found has convinced the experts.

In his search for the Mapinguari, the hunter and explorer Vernon Hesketh–Prichard travelled huge distances across these grasslands in Patagonia in the southernmost part of South America.

Who shot at a Mapinguari in 1888?

How tall is the Mapinguari said to be?

Who travelled for 900 miles (1500 kilometers) in search of a Mapinguari?

The Loch Ness monster is probably the most famous cryptid in the world. Nobody has ever proved that "Nessie" really exists—but lots of people would certainly like the stories to be true!

CRYPTID FILE

Subject	The Loch Ness monster
Length	About 26 feet (8 meters)
Habitat	Loch Ness, Scotland
Status	UNEXPLAINED

LEGENDS OF THE MONSTER

Stories and legends of the Loch Ness monster go back as far as 570 CE. For a long time, the creature was hardly known outside Scotland. But when a new road was built along the side of Loch Ness in the 1930s, many more people came to visit the area—and Nessie's fame began to spread.

EXTRAORDINARY

On 22 July 1933, a Londoner, George Spicer, and his wife were driving beside the loch when they saw "a most extraordinary form of animal" lurch across the road, leaving a trail of broken undergrowth behind it. Spicer reported the sighting to the local paper. Soon "Loch Ness monster" stories were all over the national press.

This photograph, taken in 1934 is one of the best-known images of Nessie. Unlike other pictures, it shows the creature's head and neck. The image was revealed as a hoax in 1994.

FACT OR FAKE?

Over the years many scientists have tried to find out if the Loch Ness monster really exists. One of the most thorough investigations was by the BBC in 2003, when scientists used special equipment to search the loch for unusual sounds. They found no evidence of anything bigger than a fish.

Where is Loch Ness?

Who saw the monster in 1933?

When did the BBC carry out an investigation?

Alex Campbell lived and worked for many years in the Loch Ness area. He claimed to have seen the monster 18 times.

SPECTACLE ON LOCH NESS

What was it?

A CORRESPONDENT.

CAUGHT ON CAMERA

Since the 1930s, several people claim to have photographed a serpent-like creature swimming with its head above the water. But the evidence has never convinced the experts.

One theory is that Nessie could be related to a creature known as a **plesiosaur**, which might have been trapped in the loch at the end of the last Ice Age. However, experts argue that all known plesiosaurs died out millions of years before Loch Ness was formed.

Loch Ness was formed in the last Ice Age. One of Scotland's deepest lochs, it contains as much water as all the lakes of England and Wales put together.

SNAKE OF THE WATER

Long before the first European **settlers** came to the shores of Lake Okanagan in Canada, local people told stories of Ogopogo, a terrible monster living deep in the lake.

Many believe that the Ogopogo is a plesiosaur, a giant animal that lived in the sea millions of years ago. The name "Ogopogo" comes from a Native American song.

CRYPTID FILE

Name	Ogopogo
Length	Up to 65 feet (20 meters)
Habitat	Lake Okanagan, British Columbia, Canada
Status	UNEXPLAINED

A HUGE CREATURE

On July 8, 1952, two friends were sitting beside Lake Okanagan when they saw a huge creature in the water about 280 feeet (85 meters) away. Its body was long and thin, with a horse-like head on a long neck. For three minutes, the two women watched in amazement as it splashed around in the lake before diving out of sight.

The next day, they reported the sighting to the local newspaper. Soon dozens of other people were writing in to report their own sightings.

Lake Okanagan is 85 miles (135 kilometers) long and certainly deep enough to contain a large creature. There are towns and villages on the shore of the lake, but the area around it is mostly forested and few people live there.

VANISHED

Researchers who investigated the story found there had been many mysterious incidents in the lake over the years. Swimmers had vanished; boats had been attacked. Horses tethered to canoes had been dragged underwater by an unknown force. Sometimes a large creature had even been seen rising up from the lake to grab birds in mid air.

SIGHTINGS

The sightings have continued right up to the present day. Six times a year, on average, someone reports seeing the creature. Many people claim to have photographed and filmed Ogopogo, but so far no one has ever proved the creature really exists.

FACT OR FAKE?

Ogopogo was first seen by people as long ago as the 1800s. In 1926, a large group of people in cars parked on the shore of the lake all said that they saw the creature at the same time. A local newspaper editor wrote: "Too many reputable people have seen the monster to ignore the seriousness of the actual facts."

How big is Ogopogo said to be?

Where does the name Ogopogo come from?

Where is Ogopogo said to live?

THE ORANG PENDEK

In central Sumatra, Indonesia, a strange half-human creature is said to live in the jungle. Villagers fear it. But some believe the "Orang Pendek" could hold the key to one of the great mysteries of evolution.

Eyewitnesses say that the Orang Pendek looks like a small, hairy human being. It has a human nose and shoulder-length hair, and gives a low whistle-like call.

SUPERSTITION

When British naturalist Debbie Martyr heard about an "ape-man" living in the jungle of central Sumatra, she put the stories down to local superstition. But in 1989, she had an experience that changed her life forever: she saw the creature with her own eyes!

"It was a gorgeous color, walking upright," Debbie said. "It didn't look like anything I had seen in books or zoos. I had a camera in my hand at the time, but I dropped it, I was so shocked."

FACT OR FAKE?

One theory is that the Orang Pendek could be a survivor from a "missing stage" of evolution, when apes first began to learn to walk upright like human beings. But is the Orang Pendek an animal—or a human? Until more evidence is found, no one can say.

EVIDENCE

Determined to find the truth behind the Orang Pendek stories, Debbie set out to collect as much evidence as she could. With a photographer, she traveled hundreds of miles through the jungle in the hope of seeing the creature again.

After 15 years, Debbie finally gave up her search. But deep in the Sumatran jungle, others are now carrying on the work that she began.

 Apes such as this orangutan walk mostly on all fours, but the creature seen by Debbie Martyr walked upright like a human being.

CRYPTID FILE

Name Orang Pendek
Height About 3 feet (1 meter)
Habitat Sumatra, Indonesia
Status UNEXPLAINED

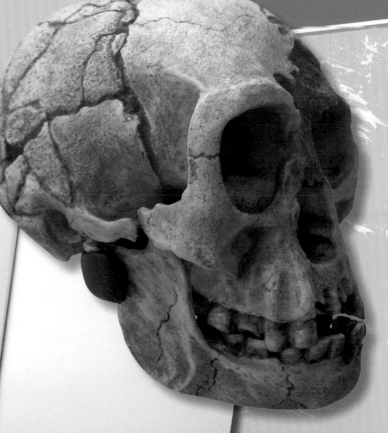

How tall is the Orang Pendek?

Where is the creature said to live?

Who spent 15 years collecting evidence about the Orang Pendek?

THE LAST DINOSAUR

Imagine traveling in central Africa and coming across a creature as scary as the Mokele-Mbembe! You would certainly want to tell your friends about it. But would they believe you?

"ONE WHO STOPS RIVERS"

In February 1932, the Scottish naturalist Ivan Sanderson was traveling along the Mainyu River in west Africa when he saw a huge dinosaur-like creature on the bank. Within moments it disappeared into the water. According to his guides, it was called Mokele-Mbembe—literally, "one who stops rivers"—and had been part of local folklore for centuries.

The naturalist and writer Ivan Sanderson made many journeys to Africa in search of rare and unusual animals.

Mokele-Mbembe was said to be between an elephant and a hippopotamus in size. It had a long neck and tail and round clawed feet like a dinosaur.

CRYPTID FILE
Name Mokele-Mbembe
Size Up to 65 feet (20 meters) long
Habitat Congo Basin, Central Africa
Status EXPLAINED

These mangrove swamps near the mouth of the Congo River have often been thought to be inhabited by strange dinosaur-like creatures.

FACT OR FAKE?

In 1919, a 32-man team of explorers and scientists set out for central Africa in search of new plants and animals. During the expedition, the team's African guides found large, unexplained tracks along the bank of a river. Later they heard mysterious roars coming from a swamp that were unlike those of any known animal.

THE SEARCH GOES ON

After Sanderson's sighting, others set out to find Mokele-Mbembe. In 1981, two US cryptid hunters, Roy Mackal and Jack Bryan, were traveling down the Congo River when they heard a loud splash and saw something in the water. Both men claim that it was "much bigger than either a crocodile or a hippo." Some explorers claim to have filmed the creature, but most of the evidence has turned out to be fake.

Could there be a large dinosaur-like creature hiding somewhere in the rivers of central Africa? It seems unlikely. Most experts now believe that Mokele-Mbembe only ever existed in legend.

Where is the Mokele-Mbembe said to live?

What does "Mokele-Mbembe" mean?

Who claimed to have seen Mokele-Mbembe in 1932?

THE YOWIE

CRYPTID FILE

CRYPTID FILE

Name Yowie
Height About 5 feet (1.5 meters)
Habitat Eastern Australia
Status UNEXPLAINED

Strange footprints in the sand? Unexplained attacks on pets and other animals? Watch out—there could be a Yowie about!

HAIRY HORRORS

When settlers first came to Australia in the 1800s, Aboriginal people had already lived there for thousands of years. The Aborigines were great storytellers and often spoke of fierce ape-like creatures called **Yowies**. They thought Yowies lurked in lonely parts of the **bush** and came out at night in search of prey.

At first, the settlers were doubtful— but it was not long before they started to think the stories might be true. Over the next century, countless people all over Australia claimed to find large footprints or see hairy, gorilla-like creatures walking upright in the forests and mountains.

This wooden statue of a Yowie is in Queensland, Australia. People who claim to have seen Yowies say they either look like large monkeys or ape-like human beings.

82

CLOSE ENCOUNTER

One person who is convinced that Yowies exist is Australian cryptid hunter Rex Gilroy. After his own close encounter with a Yowie one night in 1970, Gilroy started to collect evidence and analyze the sightings.

Gilroy's theory is that Yowies belong to an extinct type of ape. Others argue that the original Yowies were not apes at all, but Aboriginal people who were driven out of their tribe for committing crimes and who lived far away from everybody else in the **outback**.

FACT OR FAKE?

*In the 1970s many people in Australia reported seeing Yowies, but proof has always been hard to find. Recently Yowies have been blamed for attacks on household pets, but these are more likely the work of wild animals, such as **dingoes**.*

Australian cryptid hunter Rex Gilroy displays a cast said to have been made from a Yowie footprint.

The Australian outback is a vast desert area of dry grasslands and forests. There is certainly enough space for a population of apes here, but what would they live on?

Who analyzed evidence of Yowie sightings?

What species is the Yowie said to belong to?

What other theory might explain the Yowie?

THE MAROZI

Walking alone in the African bush, you find yourself face to face with a fierce creature that has terrifying teeth and razor-sharp claws. But is it a lion, a leopard— or a Marozi?

Marozi are small lions that have leopard-like markings. Similar animals have been bred in captivity, but they are rarely seen in the wild.

LION OR LEOPARD?

In 1923, a British hunter was crossing the Aberdare mountains near Mount Kinangop in Kenya, when he saw what he thought were two unusual-colored leopards. His guides told him they were mountain lions, known locally as Marozi. He later inspected the tracks, which were more like those of a lion than a leopard. Normally, lions do not live in woodland or in the mountains, but on open grassy plains.

Name	Marozi
Size	About 6 feet (1.8 meters long, excluding tail)
Habitat	Kenya, East Africa
Status	UNEXPLAINED

What two animals does the Marozi most resemble?

Where was a Marozi seen in 1923?

Who went in search of the Marozi in 1933?

 Over the years, several hunters claim to have seen Marozi-like creatures in these mountains in Kenya's Aberdare National Park.

THE ABERDARE LIONS

Twelve years years later, a Kenyan farmer shot two similar creatures in a forest in the Aberdare Mountains. He sent the skins to the capital, Nairobi, for study. The "Aberdare Lions" were found to be an adult male and female. They were slightly smaller than most lions, and had spots on the sides of their bodies and a dark stripe along their back.

WHAT HAPPENEND NEXT?

In 1933, the English adventurer Kenneth Dower organized an expedition into the hill forests to find the Marozi. He heard lots of stories, but failed to capture a Marozi alive. Sightings of the Marozi continued to be made until the 1970s. Perhaps after that, the animals became extinct.

FACT OR FAKE?

Some say the Marozi is a cross between a lion and a leopard. Others think that it is a type of lion that has somehow kept its baby spots into adulthood. Some scientists think that the Marozi belongs to a separate species of lion found only in mountain regions.

CRYPTIDS THAT COME TRUE

How many of the cryptids in this book really exist? We may never know. But there are certainly many more animals still out there, waiting to be discovered!

KNOWN ANIMALS...

Often, cryptids turn out not to exist, or just to be different versions of animals that are already known. But once in a while an entirely new type of animal is discovered.

CRYPTID FILE

Subject   Okapi
Height   5-6.5 feet (1.5 to 2 meters)
Habitat   Ituri Rainforest, central Africa
Status   RECOGNIZED SPECIES

... AND NEW SPECIES

The okapi (*oh-kah-pee*) was recognized in 1901. The coelacanth (*see-lo-canth*) was identified in 1938. The Yemen monitor lizard was identified in 1991. In each case, people in the area had been talking about the animal for years, but scientists refused to believe it existed.

 Okapi are members of the giraffe family and live in the Ituri rainforest of central Africa. They were unknown to western scientists until an explorer captured one for study in 1901.

THE SAOLA

For centuries, the saola, a type of small antelope, lived undetected in the forest regions of eastern Indochina. Then in 1991, a hunter found a saola skull in the mountains and showed it to a scientist. A team of experts visited the region, saw the saola, photographed it and captured it for study. Even now, the creatures are very rare, and only 11 have been officially sighted.

The saola is one of the world's rarest mammals. Local people call it the "polite animal" because it moves so quietly through the forest.

THE COELACANTH

The huge deep-sea fish known as the coelacanth was thought to have vanished with the dinosaurs 65 million years ago. The first living specimen was found off the east African coast in 1938. A second species was discovered in Indonesia in 1998.

When was the okapi accepted as a real animal?

Where does the saola live?

When was the first living coelacanth discovered?

A scientist examines a coelacanth caught by Kenyan fishermen in April 2001.

DISAPPEARANCES

THE DISAPPEARED

This book describes some of the most baffling and mysterious disappearances of all time. Many of them have remained unsolved for centuries.

ASKING QUESTIONS

When people or things suddenly vanish, it is natural to ask questions—and often there is a simple explanation. Maybe a crime has been committed, or an accident of some kind has taken place.

 Since the 1950s many mysterious disappearances have taken place in the stretch of ocean known as the Bermuda Triangle in the western North Atlantic.

But sometimes people vanish in **bizarre** circumstances, and there are no clues to what happened—or the clues that are left behind just add to the mystery. Occasionally, an entire ship will vanish without trace, or an aircraft will take off and never be seen again.

The British explorer Percy Fawcett disappeared in the 1920s while searching for a lost city in the jungles of Brazil.

DISTRESS SIGNALS

Usually ships or aircrafts that get into difficulties send out distress signals— but not always. When a DC4 airliner disappeared over Lake Michigan during a routine flight from New York to Seattle on June 23, 1950 no call for help was ever received. Debris was later found floating in the water, but the **wreckage** of the plane itself has never been found.

Just as baffling is the case of the three **lighthouse** keepers who disappeared on the remote Scottish island of Eilean Mohr. Inside the lighthouse, everything had been left in perfect order. The **logbook** had been kept up to date and there was no sign of anything wrong. Yet the men vanished without trace and were never seen again.

Lake Michigan in North America has been the scene of several unexplained incidents involving ships and planes.

How many answers to famous unsolved mysteries lie at the bottom of the sea?

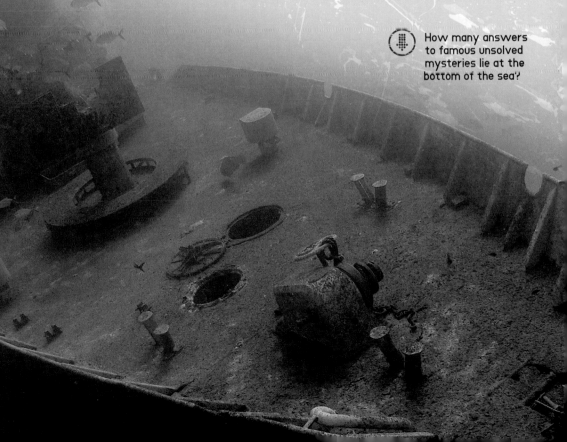

THE LOST PATROL

Over the last 60 years, the area of ocean known as the Bermuda Triangle has been the scene of many strange disappearances. One of the most mysterious was the case of Flight 19.

 The legendary "lost squadron," Flight 19, believed lost in the Bermuda Triangle shortly after the end of the Second World War.

DISAPPEARANCE FILE

Subject Flight 19
Date December 5, 1945
Place Coast of Florida, USA
Status UNEXPLAINED

LOST AT SEA

On December 5, 1945, a flight of five US Avenger torpedo bombers took off from Fort Lauderdale Air Force base in Florida, USA. The pilots were due to carry out a routine practice bombing attack at sea.

After the planes had completed the practice, the flight commander, Lieutenant Charles Carroll Taylor, exchanged several routine radio messages with base. But then his messages became stranger. Shortly afterwards, all contact was lost. The planes were never seen again.

This Avenger **torpedo** bomber is similar to the planes flown by the pilots of Flight 19. The Avenger was sturdy, easy to fly and popular with pilots.

WHAT REALLY HAPPENED?

The truth about Flight 19 will probably never be known. The official story was that the planes simply got lost and ditched in the sea. One theory is that unusual "magnetic forces" in the Bermuda Triangle may have interfered with compasses and other equipment on board the planes.

NO SURVIVORS

As soon as the aircraft were reported missing, a search was mounted. Aircraft and ships in the area were asked to watch out for wreckage and survivors. Nothing was ever found.

WHAT HAPPENED NEXT?

The US Navy launched an investigation. It was found that after the bombing practice, the planes had headed northeast to the Bahamas, but that for some reason, the flight commander had thought they were heading southwest to the Florida Keys. Instead of returning to Florida, in fact he led the planes further out to sea. The report could not explain how he made such a basic mistake. It concluded with the words "Cause Unknown."

Who commanded Flight 19?

What type of plane were the pilots flying?

What were the final words of the Navy's report?

93

LOST AT SEA

When a big ship goes down, investigators can often piece together the story of what happened by studying the wreckage. But if a vessel vanishes without trace, the mystery can remain unsolved forever.

DISAPPEARANCE FILE

Subject   USS Cyclops
Date   March 1918
Place   North Atlantic Ocean
Status   UNEXPLAINED

Some believe that the USS *Cyclops*' huge cargo of ore made her **unstable** and that she sank in a heavy storm.

One such case was the USS Cyclops, a 17,000-tonne **cargo** ship owned by the US Navy. Sometime after March 4, 1918, the ship vanished while carrying a cargo of **ore** from Rio de Janeiro in Brazil to Baltimore, Maryland, on the east coast of the USA.

All 306 of the ship's passengers and crew disappeared without trace. The Navy had lost warships in battle before, but it was very unusual for so many lives to be lost so mysteriously.

DISTURBING

At the time the Cyclops vanished, the USA was at war with Germany. Some believed the ship could have been "stolen" by its German-born captain and handed over to the enemy.

After the search for the missing ship began, the US Navy received a disturbing **telegram** from a US official in Barbados, sent before the Cyclops went missing. According to the official, the ship's captain had taken on a lot of extra coal and food, as if he was preparing for a long voyage. The official also said that many of the passengers had German names. His message ended: "I fear a fate worse than sinking."

This crew member was one of 236 officers and men who are believed to have lost their lives when the USS *Cyclops* disappeared.

How many people were on board the USS Cyclops when it vanished?

What nationality was the ship's captain?

What was the ship carrying when it vanished?

WHAT REALLY HAPPENED?

One theory, supported by the Barbados telegram, is that German passengers took over the Cyclops, killed the crew and sailed to Germany. But after the war ended, the Germans denied all knowledge of the ship. Many other theories have been suggested, but none that really solves the mystery.

95

FLIGHT INTO MYSTERY

In 1937, American pilot Amelia Earhart set off to become the first woman to fly round the world. It was a journey from which she never returned.

Aged 40, Amelia Earhart was an outstanding pilot who broke many flying records. Before her disappearance, both she and her navigator Fred Noonan had successfully completed many long flights.

EMPTY OCEAN

Just after midnight on July 2, Earhart took off from Lae in New Guinea on one of the final stages of her journey. She was bound for Howland Island, a tiny strip of land in the middle of the Pacific, where a US coastguard ship, the *Itasca*, was waiting to guide her in.

Early that morning, the *Itasca* picked up a radio message from Earhart saying that she could not find Howland Island. After this, the signals from Earhart's Electra 10E plane became fainter and fainter. Then there was silence.

DISAPPEARANCE FILE

Subject   Amelia Earhart
Date   July 2, 1937
Place   Pacific Ocean
Status   UNEXPLAINED

OUT OF FUEL

At first, people thought that Earhart had run out of fuel and crashed into the sea. Then the radio signals were analyzed. One seemed to come from Gardner Island, about 310 miles (500 kilometers) south of Howland. Later, the island was searched, and a skeleton, a woman's shoe, and a piece of **aluminum**, possibly from an aircraft, were found.

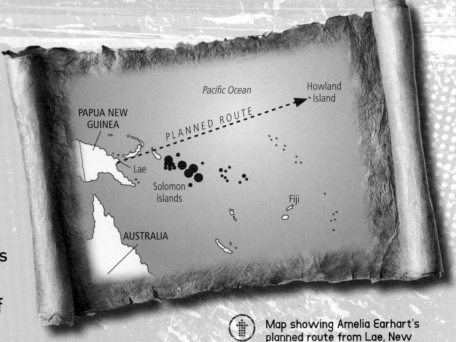

Map showing Amelia Earhart's planned route from Lae, New Guinea, to Howland Island, halfway between Australia and Hawaii, USA.

WHAT REALLY HAPPENED?

*Some have claimed that Earhart crash-landed on Japanese-occupied Saipan Island, and was later executed as a US **spy**. However, photographs showing Earhart as a prisoner turned out to be fake. Others believe Earhart is still alive somewhere under another name, but there is no evidence to support this.*

Over the years, many theories were put forward to explain Amelia Earhart's disappearance, but nothing was ever found that could be proved to be from her plane. Her case remains one of the great unsolved mysteries of the twentieth century.

What type of aircraft was Earhart flying?

Who was Earhart's navigator?

Which island was Earhart heading for when she vanished?

THE LOST COLONY

In sixteenth-century America, many settlers lost their lives in the struggle to build a future in the "New World." But could a whole community of 115 people really disappear without leaving any trace?

ON ROANOKE ISLAND

In 1585, English settlers arrived to found a **colony** on Roanoke, a small island off the coast of North Carolina. Life was hard, and the small community suffered many setbacks. But when the colony's governor left and returned three years later, he was shocked by what he found. Everyone had gone. The houses were empty, and the paths overgrown with weeds. The only clue to what had happened was a single word, "CROATOAN," carved on a wooden post.

 This reconstruction of an early English settlers' village in Virginia shows how the Roanoke colony might have looked.

DISAPPEARANCE FILE

Subject	The Lost Colony of Roanoke
Date	1587
Place	Roanoke, Virginia
Status	UNEXPLAINED

WHAT REALLY HAPPENED?

*One possibility is that the settlers ran out of food, tried to return to England but died on the journey. More likely, the survivors ended up living among nearby Native American tribes, who either adopted or **enslaved** them. Scientists and historians are now testing this theory.*

"CROATOAN"

Before he left, the governor had told the settlers that if anything went wrong, they were to leave a clue to what had happened. If they went to live with the nearby, friendly Croatoan tribe, they were to write "CROATOAN" on a tree. If they were attacked or driven out against their will, they were to carve a cross instead.

For years afterward, people tried to find out what had happened. Some reported seeing fair-skinned people on nearby Croatoan Island. Others reported seeing traces of settlements further along the North Carolina coast. To this day, no one can say for certain what happened to the Roanoke settlers.

 Archeologists excavate the site of a fort close to where the original Roanoke colony is believed to have stood.

When was the Roanoke colony founded?

How many colonists disappeared?

What word was found carved on a post at Roanoke?

THE LINER THAT VANISHED

On July 26, 1909, the luxury steamer SS *Waratah* set sail from Durban in South Africa with 211 passengers and crew. Built to carry passengers emigrating from Europe to Australia, the *Waratah* was returning to England after her second voyage.

DISAPPEARANCE FILE

Subject   SS Waratah
Date   July 27, 1909
Place   Indian Ocean
Status   UNEXPLAINED

BRIGHT FLASHES

On July 27, a ship called the *Harlow* spotted a large steamer that looked like the *Waratah* some distance away. Later, the crew of the *Harlow* saw two bright flashes on the horizon, but they thought they were caused by fires on the shore.

The *Waratah* was due to reach Cape Town on July 29. She never arrived. Naval ships searched the area where she was last seen, but no trace of her was ever found.

 Known as the "Australian Titanic," the SS *Waratah* was only one year old at the time of her disappearance. The ship did not carry a radio, but this was not unusual at the time.

PUBLIC ENQUIRY

After the Waratah disappeared, a public enquiry was held in London. Some experts said the ship might have been top-heavy; others said she could have been the victim of a freak wave or a "hole in the ocean," when winds and currents can drag even a large ship to the bottom.

Many theories were argued back and forth. The well-known writer of the *Sherlock Holmes* stories, Sir Arthur Conan Doyle, even held a **séance** to try and find out what had happened. But in the end, no one could explain how such a large ship could vanish without leaving either wreckage or survivors.

WHAT REALLY HAPPENED?

The Waratah was carrying a heavy cargo of lead which could have shifted, causing her to capsize. But if so, where was the wreck? In 1999, the wreck of a big ship was spotted in the area where the Waratah vanished, but this was found to be a transport ship sunk by a German U-boat in 1942.

 Many ships have been lost in stormy seas off this rocky **headland**, known as the Cape of Good Hope, on the southern tip of South Africa.

How many people were on board the Waratah?

What famous ship was the Waratah compared to?

Which port was the Waratah bound for?

THE MARY CELESTE

In 1872, a small cargo ship was found drifting in the Atlantic Ocean. Everything on board seemed perfectly normal, except for one thing: the ship was deserted. No trace of the crew has ever been found. The case of the *Mary Celeste* remains one of the great unsolved sea mysteries of all time.

DISAPPEARANCE FILE

Name Mary Celeste
Date November 1872
Place North Atlantic Ocean
Status UNEXPLAINED

SHIP OF GHOSTS

On November 5, 1872, the *Mary Celeste* set sail from New York bound for Genoa in Italy with a valuable cargo of raw alcohol. On board were Captain Benjamin Briggs, his wife and daughter, plus a crew of seven men.

Ten days later, another ship, the *Dei Gratia*, set sail on a similar route under Captain David Morehouse, an acquaintance of Briggs. After a month at sea, Morehouse spotted the *Mary Celeste* drifting in the Atlantic. He immediately sensed that something was wrong and sent his **chief mate**, Oliver Deveau, to investigate. Finding the *Mary Celeste* deserted, Deveau and two others sailed her to Gibraltar.

In a final letter to his mother, the captain of the *Mary Celeste*, Benjamin Briggs, wrote: "Our vessel is in beautiful trim and I hope we shall have a fine passage."

WHAT HAPPENED NEXT?

At Gibraltar, an official enquiry was held. The crew of the *Dei Gratia* were questioned and the *Mary Celeste* was examined. All the crew's clothes and possessions were still on board. The cargo was intact. The hatch on the main cargo **hold** was closed, but two smaller hatches were open. The last entry in the log was dated November 25.

A painting of the *Mary Celeste* in 1861. At this time, the ship was known as the *Amazon*.

The enquiry found that Captain Briggs and his crew had abandoned the *Mary Celeste* in a great hurry and taken to the **lifeboat**. Why they had left the ship and what happened to them afterwards was never discovered.

WHAT REALLY HAPPENED?

Over the years many people have tried to solve the mystery of the Mary Celeste. Some even claim the crew were abducted by aliens! One theory is that alcohol fumes from the cargo may have made the captain think the vessel was about to explode, and this was why he and the crew left in such a hurry.

Who was the captain of the Mary Celeste?

What cargo was the Mary Celeste carrying?

Who boarded the Mary Celeste when she was found?

THE LOST ARMY OF CAMBYSES

In the summer of 2000, scientists searching for oil in the Egyptian desert came across weapons, jewelry, and human bones buried in the sand. Could these be the remains of the lost army of Cambyses?

After crossing the Sinai desert, Cambyses' army swept into Egypt, easily defeating the forces of Psamtik III at the Battle of Pelusium.

A MIGHTY RULER

In the sixth century BCE, the Persian ruler Cambyses II was one of the most powerful men in the ancient world. After successfully invading Egypt in 525 BCE, Cambyses sent an army of 50,000 soldiers from Thebes to Siwa in the desert west of the River Nile. The soldiers' orders were to attack the Temple of Amun, where rebel priests were refusing to accept his rule.

After marching for seven days across the desert, the army were resting at an **oasis** when a fierce wind sprang up. Soon columns of whirling sand descended on the troops, burying men and animals in clouds of dust.

DISAPPEARANCE FILE

Name: The Lost Army of Cambyses
Date: 525 BCE or 524 BCE
Place: Western Egyptian Desert
Status: UNEXPLAINED

 The story of Cambyses' army was first told by the Greek historian, Herodotus (484–425 BCE).

WHAT HAPPENED NEXT?

Hearing what had happened, Cambyses sent out riders to try to find his army. The trail led through the desert oasis of Bahariya, then southwest toward Siwa, but disappeared in the sand. The huge army had vanished without trace.

For many years, historians thought the story was just a myth. But over the last ten years, important finds have been made in Egypt's western desert. These are now being studied by experts. Many believe they could hold the answer to the mysterious fate of Cambyses' army.

 Remains of the ancient temple of Amun at Siwa, in the western Egyptian desert.

WHAT REALLY HAPPENED?

Over the years many explorers and archaeologists have searched in vain for traces of Cambyses' army. The remains found in Egypt recently seem to be of Persian origin, and appear to belong to soldiers who became lost or stranded in the desert. Whether or not they belong to Cambyses' army is less certain.

When did Cambyses invade Egypt?

Which temple was Cambyses' army planning to attack?

Where have remains of an army been discovered?

Eilean Mohr off the west coast of Scotland is one of the most remote islands in the British Isles. According to local legend, it was haunted by ghosts who were determined to drive out intruders. Could this explain the mysterious case of the vanishing lighthousemen?

 Eilean Mohr is the largest of the seven rocky Flannan Isles. It rises 282 feet (87 meters) above the Atlantic Ocean, off the west coast of Scotland.

DISAPPEARANCE FILE

Names	James Ducat, Thomas Marshall, and Donald McArthur
Date	December 1900
Place	Eilean Mohr, Scotland
Status	UNEXPLAINED

DESERTED

On December 26, 1900, lighthouse keeper Joseph Moore was returning to Eilean Mohr by boat after a fortnight's leave. As Moore approached the island and looked for the usual signs of welcome, he was puzzled to see that there was nobody waiting at the **landing stage** to greet him.

Inside the lighthouse, Moore found the living quarters deserted. On the kitchen table were the remains of a half-eaten meal. An upturned chair lay on the floor. The lighthouse was empty, and its three occupants had disappeared without trace.

WHAT HAPPENED NEXT?

Alarmed, Moore returned with four others to make a full investigation. They discovered that two of the keepers must have left the lighthouse dressed for stormy weather. A third set of **oilskins** was still hanging on the hook.

The west landing stage had been lashed by gales. A lifebelt had been ripped from its mountings. But no trace was found of the lighthouse keepers, nor any sign of what could have happened to them. To this day, the mystery of their disappearance remains unsolved.

 The job of the lighthouse keepers was to keep the lamp lit to guide ships away from the rocks at night.

WHAT REALLY HAPPENED?

Some claim that the three men were carried off by a giant bird or sea creature. It is more likely that during a storm, two of the men went to check the crane on the west landing. Meanwhile, the third man saw big waves approaching and rushed out to warn them. In the confusion, all three were swept out to sea.

When were the disappearances discovered?

Who discovered the disappearances?

How many men disappeared?

DISAPPEARANCE FILE

Names   George Mallory
            Andrew Irvine
Date   June 8, 1924
Place   Mount Everest, Nepal
Status   SOLVED

 At the time of his disappearance Mallory was aged 38 and had many years' experience as a mountaineer. Both he and Irvine were well equipped for climbing at high **altitude**.

IN SIGHT OF VICTORY

On the day that Mallory and Irvine made their fateful attempt on the **summit** of Everest, thick clouds hid the mountain. But for a few minutes around lunchtime, the cloud lifted, and the two men were spotted within sight of the summit. Then they were once more hidden from view. It was the last time they were seen alive.

On June 8, 1924, British climbers George Mallory and Andrew Irvine set out to conquer Everest—and never came back. Nobody knew what had happened until Mallory's body was discovered in 1999. Could he have been the first man to climb the world's highest mountain?

At 29,029 feet (8848 meters), Mount Everest in the Himalayas is the world's highest mountain.

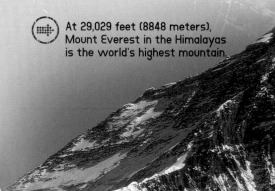

WHAT REALLY HAPPENED?

Many believe that Mallory's attempt on the summit of Everest was successful, and that he died on the way down the mountain. However, there is no proof of this. The fact that the photograph of his wife was not found on his person when his body was discovered in 1999 does not prove that he reached the summit.

MEMORIAL

When Mallory and Irvine failed to come back, their friends waited several days. Then, accepting that they must both have died on the mountain, they built a memorial **cairn** and left. The mystery of what really happened that day, and whether the two men reached the summit, has never been solved.

These snow goggles, pocket knife and watch were found on Mallory's body in 1999.

WHAT HAPPENED NEXT?

In 1933, Irvine's ice axe was found on a slope at 27,600 feet (8500 meters), but there was no sign of his body. It was not until 1999 that Mallory's frozen remains were found 850 feet (300 meters) further down the slope.

Rope marks showed that Mallory had fallen, been caught by the rope and then fallen again. A photo of his wife that he planned to leave on the summit was not in his pocket. Many people took this as a sign that Mallory and Irvine had reached the summit that day and that they were on the way down when the accident occurred.

On what date did Mallory set out for the summit?

When was Mallory's body found?

What did Mallory plan to leave on the summit?

INTO THE UNKNOWN

In 1925, the well-known British explorer Percy Fawcett disappeared in mysterious circumstances during an expedition to find an ancient lost city in the jungles of Brazil. His fate, and that of his son Jack is still unknown.

LOST CITY

Fawcett was convinced that an ancient lost city that he called "Z" existed somewhere in the Mato Grosso, a vast wooded region in western Brazil. He left behind strict instructions that, if he did not return, no one should try to rescue him in case they went missing too.

The legendary explorer Percy Fawcett was said to be the inspiration for the film character Indiana Jones.

On May 29, 1925, Fawcett sent a message to his wife that he had reached the Xingu River and was about to enter unexplored territory. The message ended: "You need have no fear of failure." Shortly after this, he headed north into the rainforest. Neither he nor his son Jack was ever seen again.

Atlantic Ocean
VENEZUELA
Amazon River
Mato Grosso
Xingu River
PERU
BOLIVIA
BRAZIL
Pacific Ocean

 Map showing the Amazon Basin and the Xingu River region, where Percy Fawcett and his son Jack were last seen.

RUMORS

After Fawcett disappeared, many rumors started to go around. Some said that Fawcett had been killed by tribespeople or wild animals; others said that Fawcett had lost his memory and was living among **cannibals**.

An explorer called Orlando Villas Boas claimed that Kalapalo tribespeople had confessed to murdering Fawcett and had handed the body over to him. But the bones were later found not to be Fawcett's.

In an interview in 1998, an elder of the Kalapalo denied that the tribe had had any part in Fawcett's death. More than 80 years later, the mystery of his disappearance is as baffling as ever.

WHAT REALLY HAPPENED?

For a long time it was thought that Fawcett had been murdered by tribespeople of the Upper Xingu River. But Fawcett took care to stay on friendly terms with local people and always took gifts for them. It is most likely that he simply got lost or died of natural causes in the jungle.

 The Mato Grosso region of Brazil has often been visited by explorers searching for lost cities.

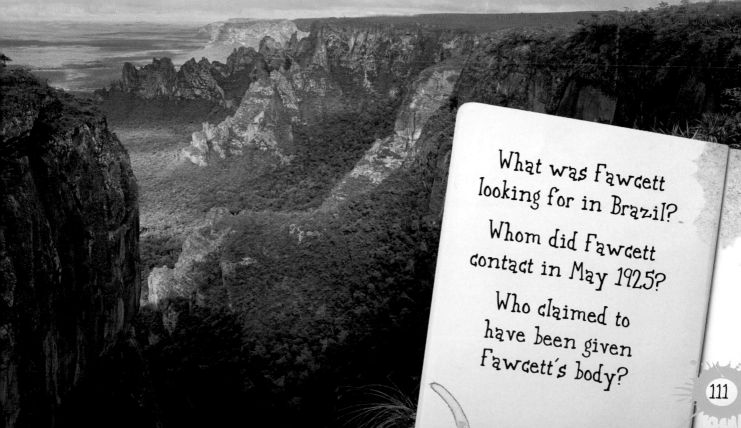

What was Fawcett looking for in Brazil?

Whom did Fawcett contact in May 1925?

Who claimed to have been given Fawcett's body?

111

Between 250 BCE and 900 CE, southern Mexico was home to one of the greatest civilizations the world has ever known. Then the huge stone buildings of the Mayan people mysteriously crumbled and their cities were reclaimed by the jungle. What happened?

DISAPPEARANCE FILE

Subject Mayan Civilization
Date 780 CE onward
Place Southern Mexico
Status UNEXPLAINED

 Mayan texts have been found inscribed on stone monuments and pottery. Some texts were also painted on a type of paper made from tree bark.

A THRIVING CIVILIZATION

Mayan civilization thrived for nearly 2000 years. The Mayans were great builders, mathematicians, and scientists. From **observatories** like the one at Chichen Itza, they even tracked the movements of the planets. Then something happened that turned their world upside down.

From about 780 CE, the Mayan cities were suddenly abandoned. It was as if the inhabitants had left and never returned. When people learned to read Mayan symbols in the 1970s, experts hoped the inscriptions would explain what had happened. They did not.

FAMINE AND DROUGHT

The mysterious decline of the great Mayan civilization has always puzzled historians. Several Mayan cities have been excavated, but no signs of warfare or violent conflict have ever been found.

For a long time it was believed that a terrible sickness attacked the population, or that a disease killed off their crops and caused the people to starve. Recently, it has been suggested that the Mayans suffered a catastrophic **drought** that caused **famine** and loss of life on a huge scale.

The Kukulkan Pyramid at Chichen Itza is one of the most important surviving remnants of Mayan civilization. Like all Mayan structures, it was built by armies of laborers without the help of machines or metal tools.

WHAT REALLY HAPPENED?

It now seems very likely that a large-scale drought could have caused the sudden collapse of the Mayan world. Scientists have looked at soil samples taken from Mexico's Lake Chichancanab. These show that in the ninth century when Mayan civilization disappeared, the region was at its driest for 7000 years.

Where was the lost world of the Maya?

When did the Mayan civilization collapse?

When did people first learn to read Mayan symbols?

THE SHIP THAT WOULDN'T DIE

In the 1920s, a small cargo steamer called the SS *Baychimo* sailed round the northern coast of Canada, delivering supplies and trading furs with local people. Then, one cold day in 1931, the Arctic ice closed in. The *Baychimo* was trapped!

ARCTIC RESCUE

Realizing he and his crew were in danger, the captain radioed for help. Soon after, the first-ever **airlift** from the Arctic took place. Twenty-two of the ship's crew were rescued. The rest decided to shelter nearby for the winter and re-board the ship in the spring when the ice melted.

 Since the *Baychimo* first drifted free of the ice, people have managed to board her several times, but nobody has ever succeeded in rescuing her or towing her safely back to harbor.

DISAPPEARANCE FILE
Subject SS *Baychimo*
Date November 24, 1931
Place Arctic Ocean
Status UNEXPLAINED

It never happened. After a severe blizzard in late November, the crew emerged from their wooden huts to find that the pack ice had loosened—and the *Baychimo* had floated away!

GHOST SHIP

Since then, the *Baychimo* has often been spotted drifting across the Arctic Ocean. In 1932, an explorer caught sight of her while sledding across the Arctic. The next year, Inuit hunters saw the ship and boarded her, but had to leave when they saw a storm approaching. In September 1935 and November 1939, the ship was spotted again near Wainwright, Alaska.
In 1962, another group of Inuit people sighted her on the Beaufort Sea.

 Inuit people live throughout the Canadian and Arctic regions where the *Baychimo* has been seen.

The last recorded sighting was in 1969—38 years after the *Baychimo* had first been abandoned.

In the early 1990s, the company that originally owned the *Baychimo* was unable to say whether the little ship was still afloat. Perhaps she is still adrift somewhere in the Arctic...

WHAT REALLY HAPPENED?

The Arctic Ocean has a pattern of circular currents that are driven by wind and by oceanic flows. These flows come in via the Bering Strait and the Greenland Sea. Once the Baychimo was caught in these unpredictable currents, it could have drifted in and out of inhabited areas, ending up almost anywhere.

What type of ship was the *Baychimo*?

When was the *Baychimo* last seen?

When did the *Baychimo* first become trapped in the ice?

GLOSSARY

Aboriginal Original tribal inhabitant of Australia.

Adapt To change in order to suit your surroundings or way of life.

Airlift An operation to rescue people by plane or helicopter.

Altitude Height above sea level. On high mountains, climbers need breathing equipment to cope with the effects of altitude.

Aluminum A type of metal.

Amphibious Able to live both on land and in water.

Apparition A visible presence of a ghostly person or thing.

Analyse To examine something very carefully.

Archeologist A person who studies the past by looking at buildings, landscapes, and evidence dug up from the ground.

Archer A person who shoots with a bow and arrow.

Baffling Very hard to explain.

Bigfoot An ape-like creature said to live in the forests of the northwest USA.

Bizarre Strange or unusual.

Bunyip A seal-like creature said to live in the Australian outback.

Bush An area of wilderness in Australia.

Cairn A pile of stones built as a landmark or to mark a grave.

Cannibals Tribal people who eat the flesh of humans for food or as part of a ritual.

Caretaker A person who looks after a place or building.

Cargo Goods carried on a ship.

Cartouche In Egyptian hieroglyphs, an oval shape that surrounds the name of a king or queen.

Chief mate A senior officer on board a ship.

Colony A community of settlers.

Creek A narrow valley with water running through it.

Crow's nest A platform at the top of a ship's mast where a lookout keeps watch.

Cryptid A creature that does not belong to a known species.

Cryptozoologist A person who studies cryptids.

Curator A person who looks after a museum or collection.

Curse To wish harm upon a person or thing.

Death mask A wax or plaster cast of a dead person's face.

Decipher To translate from code into a language that everybody can understand.

Demon An evil spirit.

Dingo A type of wild dog native to Australia.

Dispute An argument or conflict.

Distress When somebody is worried, upset, or in trouble.

Drought A time when there is no rain and crops do not grow well.

Druidism An ancient religion based on nature worship.

Electro-magnetic A type of energy sometimes said to be released by ghosts and poltergeists.

Elements Forces of the natural world, such as sun, wind, and rain.

Enslave To force a person to work very hard without being paid.

Epic A type of long poem or story about heroic deeds of the past.

Eruption The pouring out of ash, smoke, and very hot rock from a volcano.

Evolution A process by which species gradually change and adapt over time.

Excavate To dig up from the ground.

Expedition A mission to explore a place or area.

Famine A time when there is not enough food to eat.

Ferocious Fierce and aggressive.

Fiction A story that is made up by a writer.

Fiesta A Spanish word for a type of party or carnival.

Flagstone A stone slab used for paving or flooring.

Folklore Songs, stories and dances that are handed down from one generation to the next.

Forecastle The part of a sailing ship where the crew have their quarters.

Fragment A very small part of something.

Gene A chemical pattern that we inherit from our parents, which makes each of us unique.

Genuine True, real, or based on fact.

Hallucination A vision or sound of something that is not really there.

Havoc Chaos and confusion.

Headland A piece of land that sticks out into the sea.

Helmsman A person who steers a ship or sailing boat.

Henge A type of prehistoric monument consisting of a circular ditch and bank formed out of earth.

Hieroglyphs An ancient form of Egyptian writing.

Hindu A person who follows Hinduism, a religion that originated in India and is now followed by more than a billion people worldwide.

Historian A person who studies evidence from the past.

Hoax A deliberate trick or deception.

Hold The part of a ship where the cargo is stored.

Hunter-gatherers People who do not grow crops or keep animals, but obtain food from the land around them.

Intruder Someone who enters a building without permission.

Laboratory Place where scientists carry out tests and experiments.

Lagoon A type of lake.

Landing stage A place where a ship or boat can tie up safely.

Legend An old story that has often been told, but may or may not be true.

Lifeboat A vessel that passengers and crew can use to escape from a sinking ship.

Lighthouse A tall building with a light at the top to guide ships at night.

Linguist A person who studies languages.

Loch A Scottish name for a deep lake.

Logbook A written record of events.

Manuscript A book or document that is written and illustrated by hand.

Marsupial A creature that carries its young in a pouch, such as a kangaroo.

Medieval The period from the fall of the Roman Empire in the 5th century CE to the fall of Constantinople in 1453 CE.

Memorial A stone or statue in memory of a person who has died.

Miracle An amazing event that cannot be explained.

Missionary A person who travels from place to place in order to tell people about a religion.

Monastery A place where monks live.

Monumental Very big or massive, like a large stone statue or building.

Myth An ancient story that is often found not to be true.

Naturalist A person who studies the natural world.

Network A system made up of many interconnected parts.

Oasis A fertile area in the desert where water can be found.

Observatory A building from which scientists can study the night sky.

Oilskin A type of thick, waterproof jacket.

Ore Raw material from which metals can be extracted.

Outback A remote area of wilderness in Australia.

Pact A deal or agreement.

Pagoda A type of eastern temple.

Paranormal Contrary to the laws of science.

Patriotic Devoted to your country.

Pharaoh A royal ruler of ancient Egypt.

Philosopher A person who studies the meaning of life.

Plague A disease that spreads quickly and affects many people.

Plaque A memorial stone or plate.

Plesiosaur A type of prehistoric sea creature.

Poltergeist A ghost that is invisible, but can make objects move around.

Prehistoric Very ancient, dating back to a time before writing and record-keeping were invented.

Pyramid A type of huge burial chamber built for the pharaohs of ancient Egypt.

Reign The length of time a king or queen rules a country.

Resting place Where a person's remains are kept after they die, e.g. a grave.

Rigging The ropes that hold up a ship's masts and sails.

Sandstorm A strong wind in a desert carrying clouds of sand.

Sasquatch Native American name for Bigfoot.

Scalp Skin and hair covering the top and back of the head.

Scrubland An area of low-growing bushes and trees.

Séance A meeting where people try to make contact with the spirits of dead people.

Settler A person who moves to another country to start a new life.

Sighting When a person sees a ghostly presence.

Siege A military operation when an army surrounds a town.

Slave Someone who is forced to work very hard for no money.

Slave-traders People who capture or trade others to be sold as slaves.

Sloth A slow-moving tropical creature that lives in trees.

Speaking clock A telephone service to tell people the time.

Species A group of creatures, animals, or plants.

Spy A person who secretly tries to find out information.

Steamer A type of ship with a coal-fired engine.

Summit The highest point of a mountain.

Supernatural Unable to be explained by science.

Superstition Something that is believed to be true, but has no basis in fact.

Superstitious Putting too much trust in ideas which are not based on reason.

Symbol A sign or object that has a special meaning.

Telegram A type of message that is sent by telephone wires but is delivered in printed form.

Thrive To do well or be successful.

Tomb A burial place or chamber.

Torpedo A missile that travels through water and can be launched from the air.

Trapdoor A hatch cut into the floor.

U-boat A German submarine.

Unstable Unbalanced, liable to tip over.

Wombat A four-legged animal found in Australia.

Wreckage Debris left after an accident or sinking.

Yeti A large ape-like creature said to live in the mountains of Nepal.

Yowie A hairy ape-like creature said to live in the Australian bush.

ANSWERS

GHOSTS

8-9   Queen Wilhelmina of The Netherlands; 1865; "You have me at a disadvantage, Sir!"

10-11   On the battlements of the Tower of London; Henry VIII; the nephews of Richard III.

12-13   1841; Ned Kelly; 1972.

14-15   South Africa; PC Maxwell; the library's former caretaker, Robert Thomas.

16-17   Mons; April 24, 1915; Arthur Machen.

18-19   1676; Van der Decken; George V.

20-21   RCN; Villa Camila Park, Cucuta; trikinhuelas.com

22-23   Adams, Tennessee; 1817; John Bell and his daughter, Betsy.

24-25   1967; 19; with tape recorders and cameras.

26-27   At the home of Ratan Das in Kolkata, India; December 14 to 27, 2008; Rima Das.

28-29   3:25 PM; McConnell's roommate, Larkin; "Hello! Back already?"

30-31   In the north Atlantic, somewhere off the coast west of Africa; he was sick with severe stomach cramps; the pilot of Columbus's ship the Pinta.

STRANGE ANIMALS

64—65   About 5 feet (1.6 meters); Eric Shipton; Don Williams

66-67   Sasquatch; 485 pounds (220 kilograms); Roger Patterson and Robert Gimlin.

68-69   Aboriginal tribesmen; in lakes and lagoons; on the banks of the Murrumbidgee River in New South Wales.

70-71   Hans Egede; off the coast of Greenland; 65 feet (20 meters).

72-73   Ramón Lista; about 10 feet (2.5 meters); Vernon Hesketh-Prichard.

74-75   Scotland; George Spicer and his wife; 2003.

76-77   Up to 65 feet (20 meters) long; from a Native American song; Lake Okanagan.

78-79   About 3 feet (1 meter); central Sumatran jungle; Debbie Martyr.

80-81   Mainyu River, central Africa; "one who stops rivers"; Ivan Sanderson.

82-83   Rex Gilroy; ape; Yowies could be members of Aboriginal tribes who were driven out for committing crimes.

84-85   A lion and a leopard; near Mount Kinangop in the Aberdare mountains of Kenya; the English adventurer Kenneth Dower.

86-87   1901; forest regions of eastern Indochina; 1938.

ANCIENT MYSTERIES

36-37   A prehistoric monument found in western Europe; 3100 BCE; 1919.

38-39   About 13,000 years ago; a type of stone weapon; via an ice-shelf that joined Europe and America.

40-41   Hieroglyphs; French soldiers in Egypt; the French linguist and historian, Jean-Francois Champollion.

42-43   On the Greek island of Crete; in 1900; "Linear A" and "Linear B."

44-45   Egyptian priests; Thera; the Greek philosopher Plato.

46-47   "The golden one;" Hernan Cortés; Sir Walter Raleigh.

48-49   Jacob Roggeveen; Captain James Cook; 111.

50-51   Between Cornwall and the Scilly Isles in the UK; the King of Cornwall; St Michael's Mount.

52-53   c.2571 BCE; as tombs for the pharaohs of ancient Egypt; the rays of the Sun striking the Earth.

54-55   c.1250 BCE; the Greek poet Homer; the German archeologist Heinrich Schliemann.

56-57   Camelot; Excalibur; Geoffrey of Monmouth.

58-59   The Hindu god Vishnu; Indra; a giant tidal wave.

DISAPPEARANCES

92-93   Lieutenant Charles Carroll Taylor; Avenger torpedo bombers; "Cause Unknown."

94-95   306; German; a cargo of ore.

96-97   An Electra 10E; Fred Noonan; Howland Island.

98-99   1587; 115:; "Croatoan."

100-1   2.11; the Titanic; Cape Town.

102-3   Benjamin Briggs; raw alcohol; Oliver Deveau.

104-5   525 BCE; the Temple of Amun at Siwa; in the western Egyptian desert.

106-7   December 26, 1900; lighthouse keeper Joseph Moore; three.

108-9   June 8, 1924; 1999; a photograph of his wife.

110-1   An ancient lost city which he called "Z"; his wife; the explorer Orlando Villas Boas.

112-3   Southern Mexico; the ninth century CE; in the 1970s.

114-5   A small cargo steamer; 1931; 1969.

INDEX

WEBSITES

www.ghostclub.org.uk
Website of the world's oldest paranormal investigation organization.

www.ghostvillage.com
Google's most popular paranormal site.

www.nms.ac.uk/education_activities/kids_only/egyptian_tomb_adventure.aspx
Join a real-life archeologist on a mission to explore an ancient Egyptian tomb.

www.ameliaearhart.com
A site dedicated to the memory of Amelia Earhart.

www.byerly.org/bt.htm
A site about the many strange events that have taken place in the Bermuda Triangle.

www.cfz.org.uk
Website of the Center for Fortean Zoology, which organizes expeditions to search for cryptids.

http://www.newanimal.org
The website of the Cryptid Zoo.